# The Year of the Rat

# Ryan Hale

Copyright 2023 by Ryan Hale - All rights reserved.

It is not legal to reproduce, duplicate, or transmit any part of this document electronically or in printed format. Recording this publication is strictly prohibited, and any storage of this document is not allowed unless with written permission from the publisher.

All rights reserved.

Respective authors own all copyrights not held by the publisher.

About the Author ................................................... 4

Chapter 1 ............................................................... 5

Chapter 2 ............................................................. 20

Chapter 3 ............................................................. 33

Chapter 4 ............................................................. 49

Chapter 5 ............................................................. 64

Chapter 6 ............................................................. 75

Chapter 7 ............................................................. 82

Chapter 8 ............................................................. 87

Chapter 9 ............................................................. 99

Chapter 10 ......................................................... 117

Chapter 11 ......................................................... 130

Chapter 12 ......................................................... 139

Chapter 14 ......................................................... 163

Chapter 15 ......................................................... 168

Chapter 16 ......................................................... 173

Chapter 17 ......................................................... 185

Chapter 18 ......................................................... 190

Tying Up Sōngsǎn de Yīduān (Loose Ends) ......... 198

## ABOUT THE AUTHOR

Ryan Hale lives with his wife, Antoinette, in Flower Mound, Texas. They have been married for forty-four years and have three adult children and four grandchildren. They are members of a large, non-denominational church in Grapevine, Texas, and they are enjoying their retirement years.

He was a corporate manager and trainer in the restaurant business for twenty-three years. Then, he pursued a career in the telecommunications industry as a manager, trainer, and technical writer for the largest telecom in America, until experiencing a major layoff. He changed from laid off to retired and now enjoys writing and watching his grandchildren's sporting activities. *Year of the Rat* is his first book, and he is now writing the second book in the Blake Franklin Private Investigator novels. Pick up:

*One for the Money*

*Two for the Show*

*Three to Get Ready*

*Go, Kat, Go!*

*Five Will Get You Ten*

*Six Degrees of Desperation*

*Seven SEALS*

*and in 2024Eight Days a Week*

## CHAPTER 1

Reston, Virginia - May 27, 1996

A small gathering of physicians, research scientists with the World Health Organization, and a select few career politicians and economists met in a Global Achievements Reston, Virginia, office conference room. The meeting was ostensibly to discuss U.S. healthcare and its implications for the future of Medicare and Medicaid and how policy changes could serve to strengthen and save both programs. Conferences such as this one were common among Washington, D.C., think tanks, such as Global Achievements. Their outcomes often drove policy, as they generated activity through their government affairs groups.

The Virginia countryside was awash in bright green, red, and yellow colors as summer came early to the Eastern Seaboard. Reston, Virginia, is home to the high-tech corridor in the area and hosts insurance, banking, telecommunications, government contractors, lobbying firms, and think tanks. The people working in this corridor control much of the money flowing through its neighbor to the east, Washington, D.C.

Global Achievements was considered a premier think tank in the Washington, D.C., suburb of Reston, Virginia. Their K Street offices housed some of the most influential lobbyists inside the Beltway. With clients ranging from pharmaceuticals and defense contractors to tobacco and mining, Global Achievements' tentacles were entwined in nearly every piece of legislation, passed and defeated, for the past decade.

Visitors of Global Achievements went through a security checkpoint in the grand lobby of a building resembling The Crystal Cathedral in Southern California. The eight-story entry hall made a fast impression on several men and women passing through the X-ray machine while briefcases and handbags went through another device on a conveyor belt. Visitors were given blue and silver security badges to enter their assigned meeting and dining areas, restroom facilities, and communication accommodations.

Dr. Patrick Rivera, a thirty-two-year-old Doctor of Internal Medicine from Dallas, Texas, was one of those thoroughly impressed visitors. Just shy of six feet tall, Patrick wore a double-breasted navy blue suit with a light blue shirt and navy paisley tie. He thought his "corporate look" was appropriate for the occasion, though at almost three hundred pounds, the suit was a little tight, and the coat would not remain buttoned for long.

As he walked through the security checkpoint to receive his visitor's badge, he marveled at the opulence of the building and the number of armed guards and cameras present. After clipping the badge to a belt loop on his trousers, a guard directed him to a bank of elevators and a third-floor conference room he would find to his left as he exited the elevator.

Patrick entered the conference room to find six people already seated, four of whom looked up as he entered and acknowledged him with a smile or a nod of the head. An attractive woman, Patrick guessed to be in her early fifties, was one of two who did not even look at him.

She was dressed in a very stylish pantsuit - if pantsuits can be called trendy, he mused, and she exuded power and confidence in how she sat there like she was the queen of the conference. Her thick auburn hair was beautifully coiffed and showed only hints of silver that added to her attractiveness.

When Patrick did see her blue eyes, he thought they were gorgeous but steely and added to the air of superiority she so perfectly displayed. The name badge clipped to her jacket pocket read Dr. Eloise Chamberlain, CDC.

Patrick set his executive organizer binder in front of a chair next to the beautiful, icy woman. He walked to the back of the room, where coffee, juice, water, assorted bagels, and pastries were displayed. He poured coffee into a small ceramic cup with a blue GA logo on the side, added sugar and creamer, and then selected a donut from under a plastic dome. He set his coffee and donut on the conference table and sat in the padded leather chair.

"Why do they serve stale donuts at a healthcare conference?" asked Patrick of the attractive woman seated to his right. She never looked up from her binder and did not bother to shrug. He took a bite of the donut, which was like glazed air and not stale at all, then washed it down with a drink of his coffee before saying, "Ironic."

He shifted his attention to a young Asian man who had just entered, quickly surveyed the room, and chose a seat at the corner of the U-shaped conference table, where he began to unpack a small leather satchel and neatly arrange items in front of him.

Over the next ten minutes, the room filled with invited attendees until every seat was occupied, almost thirty minutes ahead of the scheduled start time. Then, finally, a man with a high, nasally voice cleared his throat, and when all eyes turned in his direction, he placed his hand on a control tablet; the glass panels surrounding the conference room frosted over, and white noise began to play within the room. The room was a SCIF or Sensitive Compartmented Information Facility, and a few attendees saw one for the first time.

The speaker was Grant Hofstetter, a sixty-two-year-old bookish man in a Brooks Brothers suit and bowtie, looking more like a local television weatherman than the Executive Project Manager for Global Achievements.

Hofstetter was handpicked to lead the initiative based on his previous experience with international healthcare, having held a position with The World Health Organization with an assignment in mainland China. After fifteen years of fruitless service with WHO, Hofstetter was recruited and assigned to form a committee that addresses the nation's most challenging political and economic issues.

"Welcome, everyone, to the first meeting of the GAP Council, Global Achievements PoliMed Council. As you can see, the room is secure, and you will notice that your pagers and other mobile devices are inoperable, and no recording is permitted within this room." Several people pulled pagers from their belts and purses and examined the screens as though they did not believe the speaker, then smiled and returned them.

"We will take frequent breaks for each of you to communicate with your staff, as we understand your importance to your respective organizations. Each of you brings something special to the table, and your contributions to our charter should be invaluable as we move ever closer to the next millennium."

He continued his introductory remarks for several minutes while Dr. Rivera sat wondering why his father had sent him to such an august gathering.

He was the youngest person in the room, except for the Asian man, whose name card identified him as Doctor Lǐ Xing Taū, a researcher. Everyone else in the room was fifty to sixty years old, and Patrick assumed much more accomplished in their fields of expertise.

Patrick was beginning his professional career after enduring many years of education and a challenging residency at Dallas Memorial Hospital. Economics was the furthest thing from his mind. He reflected on the day when his father had sat across from him in the small breakroom at his office, sorting through a stack of mail placed in front of him by a filing clerk. His father had slid an envelope addressed to Dr. Pat Rivera, lacking any junior or senior designation, and had remarked, "This must be for you. I don't know anyone in Virginia."

Patrick and a younger cousin, also named Patrick, had attended The University of Virginia, albeit five years apart. They, along with their fathers, had been given the middle name of their grandfather, the first in the family to come to America.

He had built a highly successful restaurant empire, and despite the success of the family restaurant business, his sons and three daughters had all chosen careers in medicine, a source of great pride for the elder Rivera. Even his grandchildren had achieved successful medical, surgery, and medical research careers in Dallas/Fort Worth.

Patrick was in his second year of residency when his cousin Pat earned his Ph.D. in Biochemistry. Upon opening the envelope, Patrick discovered an invitation to this conference and immediately looked forward to revisiting northern Virginia and reconnecting with friends from his college days.

Returning to the speaker with a nasal voice, Patrick caught his final statement. "It may be up to us, here in this room, to save the U.S. economy and, therefore, the global economy. Something we at Global Achievements have been working toward for more than a decade. Many of you will become an integral part of the efforts of the GAP Council as we approach the end of the millennium and beyond."

*Save the global economy?* Pat wondered how that was possible. *I'm a freaking Internist. How can I save anything but one of my elderly patients?* Rivera had recently joined his father's practice in Dallas, Texas, as the elder Patrick Rivera prepared to retire in a few years, passing on his aging patients to his youngest son.

The morning session featured three speakers who discussed the nation's health from perspectives Patrick had never considered. They explored the impact of lifestyle on the economy. How cultural changes affected the Gross Domestic Product (G.D.P.). The role of medical advancements in the inevitable decline of the Social Security System, and how targeted taxation eroded current and future wealth. Ten-minute breaks on the hour allowed attendees to step outside the SCIF for telephone calls using desk phones provided by Global Achievements.

During the second morning break, Patrick called his father to let him know he was extending his visit by a couple of days to play golf with some friends from medical school who had remained in the area.

He swiped his blue and silver badge over a card reader at the door and entered a large room with over thirty cubicles set up for guest communications. A computer monitor displayed "Global Achievements," and a small placard on the desktop warned that GA Security monitored access.

Patrick was not a computer expert and only used it to access information from news boards at home. Now running

Windows 95, his home office computer made it easier to use than memorizing DOS commands. Although he could foresee the day he and his father would need to embrace computers in their medical practice, he couldn't imagine having a significant need for them.

His father finally came on the line from his office in Dallas, and Pat was anxious to tell him all about the meeting.

"Dad, you wouldn't believe this place! We're meeting in a top-secret room, and the other invitees are like the who's who in America. It feels like rarified air in this place, for sure. I'm certain the invitation was meant for you."

"Me?" his father asked. "Why would I be in a meeting with big shots? I'm just a country doctor," he joked.

"Everybody in the room is your age, and they are all big shots, just as you said. There is one young guy from China, but…" Patrick heard a loud screeching noise, similar to the sound his home modem made when connecting to AOL, and the call dropped. The current speaker's voice came over an intercom, asking everyone to return to their seats in the conference room.

Just before noon, the meeting broke for lunch, which was served in an adjacent conference room. Patrick sat at a table set for four and was joined by John Chapman, a United States Senator, an elderly physician named Dresden, and the young Asian researcher, Dr. Taū. Patrick noticed a slight difference in the security badges hanging from the Senator and Taū's belts. Their badges were all silver with no blue borders. Looking around the room, he observed that everyone with visible badges had the same silver design and navy blue outline as his.

Senator Chapman, known for his deep, southern Bartitone voice often heard on Sunday morning news shows, spoke first. "Interesting meeting, huh?"

"You're not known for making understatements, Senator," Patrick said. "This place is like something out of Star Trek!"

Senator Chapman looked at him intently for a moment before responding, "I was referring to the agenda, not the building. I was speaking with Dr. Taū," and seemed to dismiss Patrick with a downward glance and an almost imperceptible shake of his head.

A waiter appeared to take drink orders and explained the lunch options before withdrawing. Patrick took a sip of water and noticed a stern glance from Dr. Taū. Feeling he was being assessed, Patrick asked, "Are you a golfer, Dr. Taū? Do you plan to play golf while you're here?"

"I think not. My time here is limited, and there is much work to be done," Taū responded in somewhat broken but clear English.

After enduring a full day of speakers discussing economics, GDP, the U.S. Dollar's elasticity, the gold reserve's precarious position, and various healthcare and insurance concerns, Patrick grew weary of the conference that seemed more suited for someone else.

The most engaging and passionate speaker was Dr. Anthony Foster, a Senior Research Scientist at the Centers for Disease Control (CDC). He began his talk with a brief history lesson for the attendees.

Then, he delved into the Spanish Flu pandemic of the early twentieth century, which had resulted in deaths exceeding fifty million worldwide, with over half a million attributed to the same strain of influenza in the United States.

It was a devastating virus that disproportionately affected the very young, the poor, and the elderly much more severely than it did young, healthy, affluent adults who heeded the warnings of the medical community.

No therapeutics were available at that time, and there were no suitable antibiotics to combat the secondary bacterial infections that contributed to the death toll. The only medical advice included practicing better hygiene, wearing masks, and quarantining the afflicted.

It was a terrifying narrative rooted in raw facts. However, Dr. Foster then took his talk in an entirely unexpected direction, leaving Patrick thinking Foster had lost his mind.

Dr. Foster looked at his small audience and said, "Try to imagine if this deadly strain of influenza, or some other lethal virus, were to strike the world today. In 1918, the global population was just over 1.8 billion people."

Foster continued with a fervent delivery.

"Today, the Earth is overcrowded with nearly six billion individuals, many of whom contribute minimally to the world's economies and only deplete its resources. In 1918, just under three percent of the population perished, resulting in slightly over fifty-four million deaths during the pandemic eighty years ago."

The friendly audience nodded agreeably with Dr. Foster, seemingly eating up the information he shared.

"Today, that percentage would equate to one hundred seventy million deaths worldwide. In the United States alone, we could expect to witness as many as seven million deaths!" He said this with a slight smile, turning his lips upward and widening his eyes as if delivering good news.

"Take a moment to contemplate that. Seven million individuals removed from the Medicare, Medicaid, and other entitlement program rolls." Patrick pondered this while glancing around the room, observing heads nodding and everyone seemingly inspired by Foster's words.

Foster continued speaking after a pause, allowing the impact of his last revelation to settle in.

"We have samples of the Spanish influenza and numerous other plagues that have claimed the lives of large populations globally. These samples are housed in secure laboratories in the United States and several other represented countries." Foster nodded and smiled at Dr. Taū and a woman seated across from Patrick, whose nametag identified her as "Dr. Nazanin" from the Azadi Medical Laboratory in Iran. Both Taū and Nazanin returned Dr. Foster's smile. The entire discussion left Patrick feeling uncomfortable, but Foster was not done.

"Imagine, if you will, the consequences of a new worldwide viral pandemic that doesn't claim the lives of three percent of the world's overpopulated population but ten percent instead. Is a ten percent mortality rate, a ten percent reduction in an overpopulated community, acceptable? Allow me to do the math for you. That would result in five hundred eighty million deaths worldwide. Right here in America, the death toll would exceed twenty million."

A slide on the screen behind him showed drug addicts in parks, passed out on sidewalks and lining up at methadone clinics. The people around the table shook their heads in disgust.

"Remember that we are discussing underserved communities within the medical and industrial complex and, in many cases, over-served by pharmaceuticals if you catch my drift." This was intended to be humorous, and the room chuckled politely, but Patrick was so stunned that he couldn't feign laughter.

Foster continued, "Tomorrow, we will delve into the ongoing development efforts at Dr. Taū's laboratory in Wuhan, China, and we will hear from our esteemed colleague, Dr. Nazanin, regarding the gain-of-function research her team is currently perfecting. The bottom line is this: we possess the means, the research, the funding, and the resources required to have a significant and positive impact on world economies. The question is, do we have the will?"

The slide changed and a military parade in China, juxtaposed with US Military and UN Peace Keepers with their blue helmets appeared.

"That's not for me to decide. That decision will be made at levels well above my pay grade and many of yours. This week, we are responsible for crafting an actionable plan to present to leadership. We will delve further into the details over the next four days as this highly select group, along with our hosts here at Global Achievements, has the opportunity to change the world."

The slide faded into nine boxes like the beginning of a Brady Bunch episode. In each box photos began to appear. A Man smoking, an elderly woman with a walker, a drug addict on a park bench, a poor inner-city woman with five small children, a patient in an iron lung, a small child in a wheelchair, an obese couple eating fast food and in the middle screen appeared a microscopic view of a virus, it's surface covered with spore-like shapes.

"We will explore potential impacts on specific populations that contribute significantly to morbidity and, therefore, have the most profound effects on our economies. For example, obesity is an escalating issue in this country—less so globally. Still, this particular group contributes disproportionately to other health concerns, such as diabetes, heart and lung conditions, kidney and liver diseases, as well as bone and joint problems. All of these factors artificially inflate medical and insurance costs. Dr. Chamberlain will cover this extensively on Wednesday."

Patrick noticed the woman beside him glance at Dr. Foster and nod; it was the first time he had seen her move since returning from lunch.

"I look forward to hearing from our speakers tomorrow and rolling up our sleeves to make a difference."

Dr. Foster collected his notes and smiled as the room applauded politely, everyone except for the bewildered Dr. from Dallas.

Patrick had endured as much as he intended to and decided not to return for the next four days of the conference. He had attended several medical meetings in vacation destinations like Orlando, Las Vegas, and Chicago.

These events had always included planned outings and dinners, focusing primarily on the sponsor's introduction of new drugs. Every vendor and participant had underscored the importance of saving and improving lives. In comparison, this meeting was a debacle.

He felt he had little to contribute and was gaining nothing from it. Patrick decided to rendezvous with friends and enjoy some leisure time. He never gave the Global Achievements meetings or the GAP Committee another thought. He hoped he had concealed his shock at the insane talk given by Dr. Foster, but he had a face that was easy to read.

He shook his head and muttered, "Wow! So much for 'Do No Harm.' What a sick individual," as he picked up his organizer and prepared to leave. He removed his badge and placed it on the table, recognizing that he had no further use for it, before swiftly heading to the door, crossing the impressive lobby, and stepping outside to use a pay phone to call a taxi.

The cab ride from the Global Achievements office to the hotel was impressive and scenic. Many beautiful office buildings were surrounded by manicured landscapes with ponds, reflecting pools, and fountains. It reminded Patrick of the Los Colinas area of Dallas with its glass structures and canals. Patrick enjoyed the ten-minute drive to the Marriott and remained oblivious to the silver SUV that followed several vehicles behind in the heavy traffic.

CHAPTER 2

The hotel room brightened with the sunrise as Dr. Patrick Rivera prepared for a day of golf, unaware that it would be the last day of his life. He had scheduled an eight-thirty tee time with an old classmate who had promised to invite a couple of others, making it a foursome. Patrick was eager to unwind after the highly unusual day he had experienced at the Global Achievements offices, where he had felt completely out of his element and thoroughly confused.

The previous evening, he had called his father to inform him of his plans to relax and reconnect with friends over the remaining four days of his stay, assuring him that he wouldn't extend his visit beyond the original plan. Patrick had also reached out to his cousin, who was more like a younger brother due to their close upbringing and overlapping schooling in Virginia.

Dr. Pat Rivera, a medical researcher, worked at Warner Pharmaceuticals in Richardson, Texas. His days were spent developing new therapeutics for Type Two diabetes, funded by a substantial annual government grant exceeding ten million dollars. The younger Dr. Rivera had gained recognition in critical research circles for creating an effective Type Two Diabetes treatment that eliminated the need for daily injections and had no adverse effects on pancreatic function. His approach modulated the effects of naturally produced insulin in the body. He was regarded as one of the leading research scientists in his field and currently led a team focused on developing a safe and effective weight loss medication.

Patrick showered, shaved, dressed, and retrieved his golf bag from the closet. Using a washcloth from the Marriott, he cleaned the grooves of his pitching wedge and nine iron, then examined his driver and three wood after removing the head covers.

He removed his new Calloway putter from the bag, lined up an imaginary shot, and smoothly stroked it across the thick carpet. In his mind's eye, he watched the putter sink the shot. "And the gallery goes nuts!" he exclaimed before placing the putter in the bag with the club head down.

He hoisted the bag onto his shoulder, headed to the elevator, descended to the lobby, briefly stopped by the breakfast room, and then took a cab to the Centennial Golf Club in Herndon. Patrick set his clubs next to a small table near the entrance and headed to the food Bart for a glass of juice and a bagel. To his surprise, he encountered a familiar face.

"Dr. Taū! What a small world! I didn't know you were staying here."

Dr. Lĭ Xìng Taū began to leave but stopped and greeted Patrick with a nod. "It appears you're attending another meeting today, Dr. Rivera," he remarked, glancing at the golf bag.

Feeling embarrassed at being discovered and questioned, Patrick replied, "Well, you know, the whole Gap thing doesn't interest me. I'm a doctor and not too concerned about the economy if you catch my drift."

Taū nodded and curtly responded, "Clearly. Enjoy your game." He then turned and left the hotel, getting into an awaiting SUV under the hotel's portico.

Patrick noticed a cab pulling up, grabbed his golf bag, discarded his uneaten bagel, and exited the hotel. A brief ten-minute drive took him to the clubhouse of the Centennial Golf Course, where he checked in and waited for the rest of his foursome to arrive.

Beside the clubhouse, there was a practice putting green. Since it had been six weeks since he had last played, Patrick decided to get some practice to avoid embarrassing himself with his old friend due to a rusty short game.

He took four golf balls from his pocket and placed them about twenty feet from the hole. Strangely, his hand felt damp after touching the golf balls, but he wiped his hands on a towel clipped to the bag, brushed the hair from his forehead, and scratched an unexpectedly itchy chin.

He retrieved his putter, walked to the first ball, and, with a firm, short stroke, sent the ball to within eighteen inches of the hole. Stepping over to the next ball, he took a deep breath. Despite feeling tight in his chest, he put the ball just six inches from the hole. He smiled and stepped to the third golf ball but suddenly couldn't breathe. Looking down, he realized he couldn't see the ball or the clubhouse. His world turned black, and he collapsed face-first onto the turf, dead before he hit the ground.

A silver SUV parked at the back of the parking lot inched forward slowly. As Dr. Rivera's lifeless body fell to the ground, an Asian man stepped out and casually made his way to the practice green. He picked up the putter and the four golf balls with a gloved hand and returned them to the vehicle. The SUV then departed the lot, merging into the traffic heading back to Reston.

News reports and the Virginia Northern District Coroner would later attribute the thirty-two-year-old physician's tragic death to a heart attack during a game of golf. This information would be harrowing for a renowned twenty-seven-year-old biochemist in Dallas, who had spent an hour talking to his cousin the night before when he called from the hotel to describe the strange meeting he had attended.

Two Dr. Patrick Riveras discussed all the details that the physician could recall, and the biochemist found some of the foundational points raised by the committee chairman intriguing. Firstly, the charter was rooted in the belief that America's economy would inevitably collapse due to the burden of an aging, overweight, smoking, diabetic, and generally unhealthy population. Furthermore, if the US economy were to collapse into a depression similar to that of the 1930s, it would have a cascading effect on the global economy.

Another speaker lamented the impact minority communities were having on the economy, as many of them relied on welfare and overutilized Medicaid, which was state-funded but backed up by federal grants to the states. Neither the physician nor the biochemist were well-versed in economics, but the premise seemed logical to them.

What concerned them was that this GAP Committee was determined to find a solution to the problem. Patrick was skeptical, stating, "Nobody will make significant lifestyle changes just because a DC Think tank says they should." He had laughed at the idea and told his younger cousin that he would skip the remaining sessions to play golf instead of extending his visit.

The elder, Dr. Rivera, was seeing patients when two Dallas police officers requested a private conversation. Notifying next of kin was a duty all policemen dreaded. This notification was particularly hard for Sergeant Jorge Palermo, a ten-year veteran of the force and a high school friend of the deceased Dr. Rivera. The officers followed Dr. Rivera to his private office at the back of the space and respectfully declined the chair offered. The old man stood facing them with a knot forming in his stomach.

Sergeant Palermo had never met Patrick's father when they played sports together in high school, but as the senior officer, he delivered the sad news himself. "Dr. Rivera, I'm very sorry to have to tell you that your son

Patrick has passed away," Palermo calmly said. The old man's eyes widened, and he had to steady himself with the edge of his cluttered desk. "That's impossible, officer. My son is out of town on business," he protested. "You must be mistaken," he added as he slowly sat on the edge of the desk.

"We were asked by the Herndon, Virginia PD to make the notification," said Palermo. With this added news, the old man realized his doubts and hopes were erased. Tears filled his eyes, and he felt he might lose consciousness as his lungs lost all ability to inhale.

"I...I don't understand. What happened? How can he be gone?" the old man pitifully asked.

"We don't have any details, but the preliminary report says he may have suffered a heart attack while playing golf. I'm sorry we can't be more specific. I knew Patrick personally, and I can only imagine how hard this must be. Someone will have to identify the body, and this report will provide the information you'll need," Palermo said, handing the elder Rivera a folded report that had been faxed over from Herndon PD.

The notification of Patrick's untimely death hit his father very hard. He had lost his wife to cancer three years earlier and never imagined he would have to bury another loved one. At sixty-eight years of age, he had looked forward to retiring and spending time being a grandpa to his five grandchildren. He hoped Patrick would marry his current girlfriend and produce more grandchildren. Instead, he faced the unbearable task of planning a funeral for his baby boy.

He called his office manager to his office, informed her, and hugged her as she nearly collapsed. She had been with the practice for twenty-two years, had watched young Patrick grow up, and was delighted when he joined the practice. Everyone loved him; his loss would be tough for the entire office and many patients. The staff began canceling appointments.

His nephew, Pat, volunteered to fly to Virginia to accompany his son's body back to Texas for burial. He had flown out in the late afternoon on Wednesday, the day following Patrick's death, to make the identification and arrangements for flying back with his cousin's remains as soon as possible.

Landing at Dulles International Airport, Pat Rivera took his carry-on bag and a rolling suitcase and walked straight to ground transportation, where he located the Alamo Car Rental counter. It was crowded at every position, but he patiently waited in line.

His mind kept replaying his last conversation with his cousin. He wished the conference had been more interesting to him, so he would have been sitting in a room full of physicians when he had a heart attack. However, walking eighteen holes of golf on a hot day in May, carrying forty pounds of clubs and a hundred pounds of extra weight, must have been too much for his overweight cousin.

Both cousins had joked over the years that the elder cousin needed to shed some weight, and the younger one had teased that he was working on diabetes and weight loss therapies just for his cousin's inevitable needs. He had even mentioned naming a drug after him, calling it "Chubby Riveracure," and they both had a good laugh about it.

That was six weeks earlier, at the end of March when they had played golf together. Patrick wanted to show off his new set of Callaway clubs, convinced they would shave ten strokes off his game. That day, the new clubs might have improved his game by a few strokes, but what mattered most was spending time with his favorite cousin, regardless of their performance on the course.

After arriving, Pat was called forward and rented a Toyota Camry, then drove to the Hilton Hotel in Reston, Virginia, where he had made a reservation. It was only about a mile from the Marriott where his cousin had stayed.

As he approached the hotel, a valet wearing a red vest suddenly appeared at his window. Pat handed him the key fob, and the valet efficiently took his luggage from the trunk before Pat proceeded inside. After checking in, Pat found the room and the bed to be very comfortable. However, he had difficulty falling asleep as his mind repeatedly replayed his last conversation with his cousin. He shed a few tears and agonized for a long time until finally, sleep came in the early morning hours.

Pat awoke just before eight on Thursday morning and quickly got dressed. The rental car came equipped with a Garmin GPS device, which he used to program the address for the Northern District Coroner's office in Manassas. He had made arrangements for the identification the previous day before leaving for the airport. Rush hour traffic had diminished, but it still took him forty minutes to reach the Northern District Coroner's Office in Herndon.

The building was a relic from the 1960s, with fading tan bricks on the exterior and minimal landscaping around the spacious parking lot. Pat parked his rental car on the back row, near a delivery bay with a large garage door securely closed. He walked to the front door and was buzzed in after providing his name and the purpose of his visit.

Pat was escorted to a small conference room just off the lobby. The room was furnished with old but comfortable chairs covered in gray and black checkered material.

After a ten-minute wait, a woman knocked lightly twice and entered the room. She appeared to be in her forties, thin, and stood very upright in the doorway. She extended her hand for a firm handshake as she introduced herself as Dr. Ramona Coggins, Deputy Coroner. Pat stood up from the small table and shook her offered hand.

He introduced himself as Dr. Patrick Rivera, which led to a momentary look of confusion on Dr. Coggins' face. She glanced down at a file she held at her side before asking, "Excuse me? Your name is...?"

Pat explained, "Oh, sorry. Yes, my name is the same as my cousin's. It's a family thing. I'm here to identify the body and take him home with me to Dallas."

Ramona relaxed, her expression softening as she held Pat's gaze. "I'm so sorry for your loss, Dr. Rivera," she said. "He was awfully young," she added.

Pat replied, "Yes, he is or was. Not yet thirty-three. Ironically, he recently started exercising to get in shape too. That's why his death is so upsetting and very strange," he said with an inquisitive tone. "It just doesn't seem possible this could happen."

Dr. Coggins offered consoling words, saying, "We are never really prepared to lose someone, even if they are older and have been sick for years; death is painful for the living."

Pat agreed, saying, "It is, for sure. But I mean 'strange' in that his death really makes no sense at all."

Having spoken with hundreds of family members over the last ten years, Ramona had dealt with many doubts and questions about the death of a loved one, particularly in suicide cases. Still, in her experience, death's finality was universally hard to accept. "I understand, Dr. Rivera. But, please, come with me."

They walked slowly down a corridor with dark green speckled tile and light green walls that reminded Pat of the old elementary school he had attended in South Dallas. The air smelled of antiseptic and iodine, and ceiling-mounted air cleaners hummed loudly as he followed a step behind his escort. They made a right turn, and Dr. Coggins used a scan card to open a locked door that revealed another long corridor with doors on the left and huge plexiglass-windowed rooms between them. Next to each window was a button with instructions printed on a white label to *Press Just Once Please*. Dr. Coggins pressed the button when they stopped at the fourth window in the hallway.

A young man pulled back the curtain covering the window inside the room, and a light blue sheet-covered figure lay on a gurney before him. The gurney was turned sideways, so the entire figure filled the large window. The young man walked to the head of the bed and then looked at Dr. Coggins.

"Are you okay?" she asked soothingly. Pat responded that he was and braced himself to do what he had come to do without letting emotion get the better of him. The coroner turned to the young man waiting by the bed and nodded, and the sheet was pulled down, revealing the face of Pat's favorite cousin. A sob escaped him, catching him by surprise.

"Oh, dear God," he said, reaching for the windowsill to steady himself.

"It's okay, Dr. Take your time. I know how difficult this is for you." Dr. Coggins placed a reassuring hand on Pat's shoulder as he removed his glasses and used a sleeve to dry the tears that flowed despite his best efforts to control them. She retrieved a small travel pack of tissues from her pocket, handed two to Pat, and he thanked her before passing the package back to her.

"It's him. That's Patrick. It's my cousin," he spoke in clipped sentences through tears and choked breaths. "I can't believe this is happening, but it's him, undoubtedly."

"Would you like a moment alone, Dr. Rivera?" asked Ramona.

"No, thank you. I'm good. It's just harder than I thought it would be. I can't believe he's dead," he said, looking her in the eyes and then asking, "Do you have time to answer some questions?" Pat inquired as he dabbed a tissue to his eye and put his glasses back on.

"Absolutely. Let's return to the conference room, and I'll explain the process of releasing your loved one. I can also help with clearance for the airline if you need it."

With that, she turned and nodded, and the young attendant beyond the plexiglass raised the sheet over the body before walking over to pull the curtain across the window, marking another act of finality.

Pat talked with the coroner for the next ten minutes, receiving a cursory briefing on his cousin's cause of death. He had already been informed that it was a fatal cardiac event, likely brought on by the extra weight he carried and the strain of walking a golf course in the heat of the day.

More profound questions remained unanswered and were not openly shared outside official channels. However, Pat did learn the name of the golf course where his cousin had played his final round of golf: Centennial Golf Course, located fifteen minutes away from the Virginia Northern

District Coroner's Office and the next stop for Pat before returning to his hotel.

## CHAPTER 3

Pat drove his rented Toyota Camry down a picturesque highway, with a quiet and scenic park to his left and a series of fairways and greens of the Centennial Golf Course to his right. He pulled into the crowded parking lot and was surprised to see so many people golfing in the middle of the day on a Thursday. He thought to himself, *Must be a lot of doctors in the area.*

Finding a parking place just vacated near the front of the Clubhouse and Pro Shop, Pat parked and walked in. As he entered the Clubhouse, immediately to his left was a hallway with two informational signs engraved on wooden planks with gold lettering that read *Restrooms* on the right sign and *Putting Green* on the left. Pat mentally noted it and proceeded to a glass counter straight ahead.

On the right side of the large octagonal room was a door to the locker rooms and two glass doors that led into the Pro Shop. A sign on the wall offered beginner and intermediate lessons with the resident Golf Pro, Greg Landers. Pat moved to the glass counter and waited while a foursome signed credit card slips and retrieved keys to two golf carts before exiting the side door near the putting green.

"What can I do for you?" came the greeting from a friendly man in his late sixties standing behind the counter.

Pat stepped forward, introduced himself, and said, "I'm not golfing today. I just want to ask about something that happened here on Tuesday."

"You a reporter? Cop?" the old man asked, still friendly but curious.

"Neither," Pat said. "I'm family. The man who had the heart attack was my cousin."

The man behind the counter was weathered from the Virginia sun, lean and muscular with very little excess weight. He wore a pale teal golf shirt and khaki shorts that revealed strong legs from years of walking eighteen holes several times each week.

"That was awful, son. I'm really very sorry for your loss. We've had a couple of heart attacks and a stroke or two through the years. Had our share of people who couldn't get out of the way of a poorly struck golf ball. But this is the first fatality we've had in the twenty-eight years I've been here."

Pat let that information sink in and sensed the sincere empathy the man was feeling.

"I don't know why, but I just wanted to come here and see where he died, you know, just take a look."

Pat looked around, and the old man nodded his understanding.

"I promise not to get in anyone's way, and I'll stick to the cart paths if you'd let me walk out to the hole he was on." Pat could feel the emotion starting to well up behind his eyes, and he cleared his throat and sniffed to hold back tears.

The old man introduced himself as Chain McLarney and reached a strong hand out to shake the hand of the bereaved cousin of the man who died at his golf course.

"Chain?" Pat said, inquiring. "Is that a family name?"

The old man laughed and said, "No, that's a nickname I earned back when I was young and dumb. I was a chain smoker until my early thirties, and the name stuck, even after I quit and took up golf and got healthier."

Pat nodded as though that made perfect sense to him. "Do you think it'd be okay if I walked the course to where it happened, Chain?"

"Well, that's the thing - and you can walk wherever you want to out here, son. Nobody would mind, even a little bit. But your cousin hadn't started a round of golf yet. In fact, he had just checked in for his tee time. He was waiting for the other fellas to show up. He walked out that door over there to the putting green for a bit of practice. I had two groups of four going off before his group's time at eight-thirty, and the first group was who found him and came back in here to call an ambulance."

Chain pointed down the hallway to his right and then rubbed his white hair back off his forehead.

"You're saying he never even walked onto the golf course?" Pat asked with surprise. "He was putting when he died?"

The old man shook his head yes and said, "That's exactly what I'm telling you, son. He was cheerful and smiling, carrying a new set of Calloway's he was very proud of and walked out that door. And his ticker took him a couple of minutes later. I can tell you, that's the damnedest thing ever to happen here."

While sitting with the coroner, Pat had read a copy of the EMT report that stated the patient was deceased at the scene, and all efforts to revive him had failed. They transported him to Herndon Methodist Hospital, where an ER physician pronounced him dead. Patrick was then transported to the Northern District Coroner's Office, where an autopsy was performed and confirmed that he had died of a massive heart attack and very likely had died almost instantly.

Toxicology showed that Patrick was on Metformin, so he evidently was already diagnosed with diabetes or was taking it to help him lose weight. The contusion on his right cheek had been caused by falling on a golf ball face-first, which had shattered his right cheekbone but had not contributed to his death.

Pat stood there in disbelief, trying to imagine the horror of feeling your heart give out, and quietly prayed that he didn't suffer even in the instant it took for life to leave him.

"Thank you, Chain. I appreciate your taking the time to talk to me about this," Patrick said as he was about to turn to leave. "Did his friends make their tee time?" Pat asked, not sure why he cared.

"Funny thing, that. The other three didn't show up at all, but I'm sure nobody would've played anyway. I never really thought about that until now. That morning was a might stressful."

"I'm sure it was," Pat said, and more questions began filling his mind. He shook hands again with Chain McLarney and wished him a good day. He turned and walked to the exit door and was almost there when he turned and asked,

"Did you hold onto the clubs?" he asked.

"Clubs?" Chain replied.

"The new Calloway's. Did you or someone here at the club hold onto them?"

Chain looked a little puzzled, and he thought for a moment before saying, "Let me check in the Pro Shop for you. That's where they would've been taken if we did. I was out there when the ambulance guys loaded him up, and I know they didn't take them," he said as he walked across the lobby to the Pro Shop where he opened a glass door and strode through. He returned a minute later carrying the red, white, and blue Calloway bag.

"Here you go, son. Someone must have picked them up and turned them into us."

Pat's cousin had only used the clubs a few times on Dallas area courses, the first time was with himself, as the two cousins had played one Saturday in late March. Patrick didn't have a chance to use them in Virginia with his college buddies, none of whom bothered to attend the golf date Patrick had arranged the night before.

Patrick had the contact information for several funeral homes in the area provided by Dr. Coggins at the Coroner's Office. It was a Virginia Commonwealth requirement and an FAA guideline that bodies being transported must be embalmed, so Patrick left the Centennial Golf Course and drove where his rental car's Garmin told him to go.

Forty minutes later, Pat found himself sitting in a large waiting room just off the lobby of a funeral home. Grieving family members of an elderly woman walked back and forth, hugging and consoling one another.

The mood was somber, as the event would dictate, but occasionally small bits of laughter could be heard as stories were shared and long-separated family members reunited and embraced. Promises to stay in touch were made, and the great-grandchildren of the woman in the coffin ran around as though they were unaware of the loss the adults were feeling.

James Biederman was the Director of Funeral Pre-need Services for Manassas Area Funeral Corporation. He was short and stocky with a look of a former high school wrestler, with an iron grip for a handshake.

Pat had made the arrangements for his cousin's body to be picked up from the Northern District Coroner's Office and made ready for the trip back to Dallas in the belly of an airplane. He put the fees on his credit card and included the transport costs for the trip to Dulles International Airport, as well as for an associated funeral home in Dallas that would be picking up the coffin at Love Field when it arrived.

Pat was impressed with how thorough and professional Biederman was and how easy he made the experience for Pat. Biederman had just the right tone and demeanor to deal with the bereaved, Pat thought, as he shook hands again before leaving.

Pat drove the fifty minutes in early afternoon traffic to get back to the hotel where he planned to have dinner in his room and relax until he could clear his mind enough to get some sleep. Grief had prevented sleep from coming since he received the news of his cousin's untimely death.

He pulled under the portico and handed his key fob to the valet who appeared at his window.

"Welcome to the Hilton, sir. Are you staying with us or dining?" a polished young man in his twenties asked.

"I'm staying, thank you," Pat replied as he began walking towards the entry.

"Excuse me, sir, do you want your clubs left in the car?" the valet asked.

"Sorry, I forgot. No, I'll take them up with me," and he put them over his shoulder and walked in with not just the heavy clubs but the weight of the world on his shoulders. He walked across the hotel lobby, straight to the bank of elevators, which he rode to his room on the ninth floor.

He never noticed the silver SUV that had followed him from the Coroner's Office to the Centennial Golf Course and the Manassas Funeral Home and had followed him through heavy traffic back to his hotel.

The Asian man who had walked into the Hilton lobby was not noticed either. He entered one of three GTE telephone booths on the far side of the lobby and watched as the elevator with a lone occupant ascended to the ninth floor. He then exited the phone booth and the hotel.

Pat took a shower to wash off the smell of death he felt he had picked up at the Coroner's Office and Manassas Funeral Home. He still smelled lilacs from the floral arrangements outside the parlor where the elderly woman lay in state. The shower was hot, and the hotel-provided soap and shampoo erased the unpleasant fragrances of the day.

He put on boxers, gym shorts, a University of Virginia tank top, and flip-flops, not intending to leave his room for the evening. He picked up the remote and, having second thoughts about watching television, tossed it to the bed and walked over to the desk. He picked up a pen, slid a Hilton-embossed notepad over it, and began writing down some questions he wanted answered before his flight back to Dallas.

After calling his uncle to discuss the arrangements he had made to fly Patrick's body home and giving him the address for the receiving funeral home, Pat made a call to the Centennial Golf Course. After speaking briefly with a Pro Shop employee who answered the phone, he was transferred to the front, and Chain McLarney answered with more exuberance than expected for so late in the day.

"Chain here. What can I do for you?"

"Hello, Chain. It's Pat Rivera. We spoke earlier today about my cousin."

"Sure, sure, I know you, son. What do you need? Name it," Chain replied.

"Well, sir, I was hoping you could give me the names of the other three guys in my cousin's foursome. I know they didn't show up, so I would like to be sure they know what happened and about funeral arrangements." Most of that was true, and Pat felt a little guilty for lying to this kind old man.

Chain said, "Let me just pull out this reservation book here, and here we go."

Pat wrote as Chain provided the names of his cousin's golf buddies; he even had a telephone number for one of them. Pat thanked him profusely and disconnected.

Pat was successful in reaching the friend who had provided his telephone number to the golf course. Through that contact, he gained the third person's contact information, but when he called the number for Bart Kroonenberg, the message said he was out of the calling area. He arranged to meet the other two for dinner the following evening.

Patrick set his notes aside, lay on the bed, stretched out, and closed his eyes. He could block out the waning light from the Virginia late afternoon sun, but he couldn't block out the thoughts of his cousin dying alone on a putting green at such a young age.

His uncle had made a comment on the telephone a little earlier about the irony of being at a healthcare conference trying to save the world and then having a heart attack while playing golf.

Pat had not bothered to correct his uncle by telling him Patrick had died before ever walking onto the golf course. He was practicing putting. With that thought, Pat got up, went to the Callaway golf bag in the closet, and carried it over to the bedside.

He sat down, started looking through the clubs, and discovered the absence of the putter his cousin had last used. He moved the golf heads aside one by one and removed a few covers but found no putter in the bag. *That's weird*, he thought.

He walked over to the desk and called the Centennial Golf Course. The Pro Shop attendant answered again, and Pat asked for Chain, only to learn he had left for the day.

"Is there anyone else that can help you? Did you need to make a reservation?"

Pat explained, "No, I was hoping to ask about a set of golf clubs that my cousin left when he passed away a couple of days ago."

The attendant, whose name was Carrie, said, "I'm so sorry about your cousin, and unfortunately, his clubs were picked up today."

Pat said that he was the person who picked them up that day, but the putter seemed to be missing.

"Yeah, we noticed that too!" said Carrie. "We thought that it was weird that he was on the putting green without a putter. He has...had a very nice set of clubs, but considering what happened, we were not as concerned about the missing club as, well, you know," she offered.

"Oh sure, I understand," Pat said. After an awkward silence, Pat said, "Thanks anyway," and was about to hang up when he asked, "Do you have security cameras there?"

"We do in the Pro Shop, and some are in the parking lot. What were you looking for?"

"I was hoping there would be one over the putting green. Oh well. Thank you, Carrie."

The next day, Pat waited to hear from the Coroner and the Funeral Home that everything was taken care of, and his cousin was ready to travel back home. They had not said how long it would take, but since it was Friday, he guessed they would try to get everything cared for before the weekend.

He went a little stir-crazy sitting around his hotel room, so he went to the exercise room and worked up a terrific sweat. He lifted a little, ran five miles on the treadmill, and sat in the sauna for twenty minutes. He capped it off with a leisurely swim in the indoor pool.

He was drying off when an Asian man walked into the pool area, looked slightly surprised, and then walked back out. Pat looked behind himself to see what had surprised the man, but nobody was there.

Pat sat poolside until a woman pushing a stroller and two small children in tow came in. Though the laughter of children was emotionally lifting, it made it harder to think and prepare for his dinner that evening with the people who failed to show up on the day his cousin died.

Pat showered, shaved, and dressed for dinner at The General Lee Restaurant, which was chosen by Randall Bogus, one of Patrick's school friends. He called the valet stand, and his car was waiting for him when he came down ten minutes later.

The drive to dinner took thirty minutes with the Friday evening traffic of late commuters and early diners. Reston was a bustling enclave in Virginia's power belt. Pat arrived at the restaurant, parked in the side lot, and walked around to the front entry. The sweet smell of beef cooking filled the night air.

Pat gave his name at the host stand inside and was taken to a table where two men and a woman sat waiting with cocktails. They stood, handshakes were shared, and introductions were made.

Randall Bogus was the tallest of the group at just over six feet tall. He carried a little more weight than he should have, and his thinning hair was turning grey at the temples. He looked ten years older than the rest of the group and his late cousin. He wore a dark blue pinstriped suit, a white shirt, and a pink paisley tie. His black leather shoes were polished to a bright shine with a small smudge on the toe of his right.

Randall was a close friend of Patrick's all through college, and they had remained close since Patrick left for medical school. Randall began his career as a broker and later as a lobbyist. In the latter capacity, he had become friends with Joseph Lewellen and Bart Kroonenberg.

Joseph Lewellen was the shortest of the group at five foot eight and was athletically built. He had been a shortstop in high school and still played softball several nights a week. His khaki pants had pressed pleats, and his button-on suspenders were visible when his burgundy sport coat opened. His tie was tan and burgundy paisley, and his loafers were camel-colored leather with no attempt at shine.

His wife Deandra was slightly taller than he, and her two-inch heels exaggerated the height difference. She was stylishly dressed in a blue pantsuit almost as dark as Randall's, with a white silk blouse and a gold brooch on a thin, gold chain around her slender neck.

The other no-show golfer was Bart Kroonenberg, an aide to a United States Senator traveling with the Senator out of the country. Bart was also a no-show for dinner, and Pat explained that he had received a message when he called that Bart was out of the country. Randall said it had been disconnected when he tried the number that morning.

Cocktail refill orders were taken by a server stopping by to describe the daily specials and asking if anyone else would be joining the party. Pat ordered a Diet Coke and retrieved a honey biscuit from a basket left by the server.

Pat sensed that the group was relaxed and decided to ask the question he had been waiting to answer.

"I'm curious about something, and I hope you can tell me. When my uncle talked to Patrick the night before he died, he said Patrick was meeting all of you to play golf, and he was blowing off a medical conference to do it. He said there was a tee time set up and everything."

Pat wanted to see if these people, especially Randall, the one his cousin called a friend, would be honest with him.

The two men nodded yes, and Randall spoke first. "That's right. We had an eight am tee time."

"No, it was eight-thirty," Joseph corrected. "I know because I had a seven o'clock call with my broker, and I wanted to be sure I had enough time."

"Yeah, you're right," Randall said. "It was eight-thirty. Way too early for me usually, but to see Patrick again and hang out with this knucklehead," he said, motioning toward Joseph, "I can force myself out of bed early." There was a little nervous laughter that was very uncomfortable under the circumstances.

Pat followed up with, "I'm sorry, but I have to ask. If everyone was up for the game and ready to go, why didn't you show up that morning?" he leaned onto the table with his elbows. "What happened to keep all three of you away?"

They looked back and forth at each other, and Pat, and Joseph said, 'Patrick canceled. I have no idea why. Bart said Patrick's conference was running an extra day, and he couldn't make it."

Randall affirmed this with a nod of his head. "Yeah, that's what he said. Something about the Eco conference..."

Joseph interrupted with, "Medical conference. He said the medical conference."

Pat looked back and forth between them and asked, "Patrick said a medical conference to you, Randall, and to you, he said it was an Eco conference? What does that even mean? Eco? Ecology? Economy? What is that?"

Randall said, "Economics is what he said. But by he, I mean Bart. I never talked to Patrick. It was Bart who called to cancel the golf outing."

Joseph again shook his head in the affirmative and said, "Me too. I only talked to Bart. He said the medical or economics meeting took longer than expected and that golf was out on this visit, but there would be others."

Patrick asked, "Who initially set up the golf outing." He wanted to know if it was Patrick or Bart who called everyone and found that it was Patrick who personally called Randall. Then Randall had called Joseph and Bart to make it a foursome. He didn't give it any thought that Bart was helping Patrick out by letting the others know the golf date was off.

Pat began giving the whole matter a lot of thought, and when the night ended, he drove back to the hotel with additional questions that must be answered.

CHAPTER 4

Pat had messages waiting when he returned to the hotel the previous night. One is from the Northern District Coroner's Office, one is from James Biederman at the Funeral Home, and one is from C. Darling. It was too late to return calls, and he had no idea who C. Darling was.

He set a wake-up call for six the next morning and went to the lobby for coffee and juice, then over to the exercise center to get a run-in before he started his calls. He was very methodical in everything he did, which he knew was critical to his success as a medical research scientist. He arrived at every hypothesis after scrutiny of all provable facts, eliminating possibilities until he finally arrived at the only possible true answer.

At that point, what he had to admit to himself had begun to be an investigation; the only facts he knew to be true were that his cousin Patrick was dead, and his demise came way too soon and way too suddenly. He also knew that circumstances leading up to and occurring after the apparent heart attack seemed a little murky. Why had Bart canceled the golf outing with the others? Where was the missing golf club?

Pat got a good workout, running five miles while watching a morning news program on a large television and resting on a stand in the corner. One of the stories that caught his attention was about a US Senator for the Commonwealth returning from a fact-finding trip to China.

Senator John Chapman had flown to Beijing to meet with Chinese Industrialists and Commerce Officials in the Chinese Communist Party (CCP) about expanding their factories to America, with possible incentives to move operations to Virginia. The Industrialists with whom he met were Dr. Ling Tang Chow and Dr. Fang Hong, Directors of two of China's largest pharmaceutical firms.

Pat was aware of both of these men, and it was interesting that a United States Senator would meet with them, considering the controversial work both of their companies had been doing. Both had been accused of testing their drugs on unsuspecting workers in Shanghai and political prisoners.

Neither accusation had been refuted in any way. It was also interesting that the Senator had flown to China and returned in four days. A rapid turnaround so it must have been a crucial meeting. He was confident that his cousin had said Senator Chapman had attended the meeting on Monday.

After the workout had finished, Pat returned to his room to shower, began returning calls, and made certain his travel plans for himself and his cousin's coffin were all set with Southwest Airlines. His first call was to Dr. Coggins at the Coroner's Office. A voice recording answered and stated the normal business hours for the Northern District Coroner's Office and told him the offices were now closed. It finished with an option to reach the office directory to leave a message. He listened intently before entering the numbers two-six-four for the letters C-O-G, and the voice of Dr. Coggins picked up on the first ring.

"Dr. Coggins, good morning! Thank goodness you're there on a Saturday. It's Pat Rivera returning your call."

"Dr. Rivera, thanks for returning my call but everything was cleared up yesterday."

"Please, it's just Pat. Cleared up. I'm sorry, was there an issue?" Pat asked.

"Yes. We received a call from The Manassas Funeral Services group to arrange pickup, but the service that showed up was from Jenkins Funeral Home, so I was trying to get it straightened out. However, I received a call from your attorney, and he cleared everything up, so we released your cousin's body to Jenkins. So, no issues."

Patrick sat up straight in his chair,, and the hair on his neck did as well. "What attorney called you?" he asked.

"Mr. Zhi, I believe, was his name. Is there a problem?"

"I certainly hope not. I'll call Jenkins and Manassas Funeral Home to see. Maybe Jenkins is just doing pickups for Manassas." Pat said hopefully.

She responded, "I didn't understand that was the case. It was put to me as a definite change in plans on your part. That's why I called, but by the end of the day, we were required to release the body to the funeral home for embalming purposes for the body to be transported by air. I'm very sorry if this creates a problem, Pat."

The next call was to Manassas Funeral Services, and Pat's frustration was obvious when he asked to speak with Mr. Biederman.

"James Biederman, may I help you," came the soothing voice after a brief delay.

"Biederman, this is Dr. Rivera. What the hell is going on with my cousin's body?" Pat sounded a little angrier than frustrated.

"I beg your pardon, Dr. Rivera. Can you refresh my memory a bit?"

Pat settled himself and said, "I was there two days ago to discuss my cousin, Dr. Patrick Rivera, who died on Tuesday and was to be picked up from the Northern District Coroner's Office and prepared for a flight back to Dallas."

The Funeral salesman cleared his throat and said, "Oh, yes. Of course, Dr. Rivera. I remember our conversation, and we had an affiliate do the pickup to meet your new directive. Everything has been handled in just the manner you requested through your attorney. We even expedited the cremation to…"

Pat interrupted with outrage, "Did you say cremation? Is that what you said?" he demanded.

"Yes. As I said, just as your attorney directed and we have the cremation order signed by you and faxed to our office. That was the reason for my call yesterday afternoon, but we had to proceed to meet the timeline you gave us. I assure you we followed your directives to the letter."

Pat was boiling inside, and the buildup exploded over the next thirty seconds of the call before he hung up in total disbelief. How could he fly home and face his entire family who waited there to say their final goodbyes? How could this have happened, and who the hell is this mysterious attorney that created this mess? Pat had no idea who this Mr. Zhi was, and at that moment, he recalled the Asian man who had walked into the pool area and turned quickly around and exited.

Pat's next call was to find out who C. Darling was and what he had to do with all of this. With any kind of luck, he could answer some of the questions for which Pat had to find answers.

A quiet female voice answered on the third ring. "Hello."

Pat was confused and said, "This is Dr. Rivera returning a call to Mr. C. Darling. Is he there?" The voice said, "this is C. or Carrie. I work at the Centennial. We spoke on Thursday."

Pat registered the voice and felt at ease and asked, "What can I do for you, Carrie? Did you find the putter?" he asked hopefully.

"Well, sort of," she said. "After you called and asked about our security cameras, I decided to go back and look at the parking lot footage after we closed. One of the cameras points toward the main entry, from the far-right corner, and it picks up the right side of the putting green near the door and the gate from the parking lot." She explained.

"Okay. So did you see what happened to the putter?" Pat asked.

Carrie said, "I saw more than that, and I'm not sure what to do about it. Sir. I saw your cousin die. One second, he was standing there practicing, and the next he was laying there. It's kind of grainy, but just knowing what happened. I mean, it was horrible," and she started to cry.

"Carrie, where is the video tape you watched?" Pat asked.

"It's on the shelf next to the recording deck in the Pro Shop office. They change them every morning and the next week they record over themselves."

Pat stood up and said, "You have got to get that video and set it aside for me."

Carrie met his sense of urgency with her own, "I'm leaving for work in a few minutes, and I will ask Chain to get it out as soon as I get there."

"Thank you, Carrie. By the way, did you see what happened to the putter? You said in the video that my cousin was putting – did you see it?" Pat asked.

"Well, sort of. The video is not real clear from that distance like I said, but it looked like another golfer took it." She explained.

"Oh. One of the golfers that found my cousin unconscious?" Pat asked.

Carrie replied, "No. This was someone leaving They pulled up in a light-colored car by the gate and a guy got out and walked onto the putting green, picked up the putter and left. He didn't check on your cousin at all. Kind of callous I think."

"Kind of criminal, I think," Pat responded. "Carrie. Get that tape. I will leave here in ten minutes and meet you at Centennial." I need to see it and possibly show it to the police!"

Pat called down to the valet stand and asked that his rental car be brought around. Then he went through his luggage and found the report he needed. He called the number on the top letterhead and asked for the Detective who had faxed the death notification to the Dallas Police Department.

Detective Sergeant Gary Saunders was a sixteen-year veteran of the Herndon Police Department and had worked his fair share of cases, both in Homicide and previously in The Burglary Division. He answered on the first ring, "Homicide – Saunders."

"Detective Saunders, this is Dr. Patrick Rivera. Good morning, sir, I…"

"If this is supposed to be a prank call, you're messing with the wrong guy, dumbass," Saunders said after almost choking on his coffee.

Pat, realizing the confusing context for the Detective, said, "I'm sorry, Detective. The deceased Dr. Rivera is, or was my cousin. I'm here to claim the body and fly my cousin home for burial."

The Detective cleared his throat of coffee and said, "Sorry for your loss. What can I do for you, Dr. Rivera? This isn't really my case any longer because it isn't a homicide."

"I'm not so sure it's not," Pat said. He added, "I have some interesting information that might change your mind about that."

In his years investigating death, Saunders had spoken with dozens of families who couldn't accept the Medical Examiners report and findings on the cause of death. Suicides were especially difficult. Strange accidents or natural causes were often in dispute as well.

"Look, Dr. Rivera, I mean no disrespect with you being a physician and all, but the Medical Examiner's report on your cousin is clear. Heart attacks kill people every day, sometimes even young guys."

Pat didn't bother to correct the Detective's assumption that he was a physician, and instead, he focused on what he had found as an experienced researcher. Too many anomalies were stacking up against the simple heart attack hypothesis for him to accept it on blind faith, or a Medical Examiners report.

"Did you know that his putter was missing, Detective?" Pat asked.

Annoyance began to build, and the Detective answered, "No, I didn't. And I no longer work Burglary or deal with lost or stolen property. What's your point?" Saunders asked, and he was getting close to hanging up. His experience dealing with family members in crisis was all that kept him from ending the call.

"Look. Dr. Rivera. I can only imagine what you and your family are going through right now but trust me when I tell you. The unfortunate fact is your cousin died of heart failure on a golf course. That sort of thing happens all the time. If a golf club got lost in the hubbub, what can I tell you? It isn't a priority when there is a body, and he was definitely not killed by a putter. He died because it was, unfortunately, his time. Bad ticker. Bad luck. Bad Karma. Call it what you will. It wasn't a homicide." His tone had that air of finality to it.

"Hold a second, Dr. Rivera," said the Detective when someone handed him a note, which he read.

"Dr. Rivera. Where are you right now?" he asked.

"I'm in my room at the Hilton in Reston, but I would very much like to meet with you. Can I come by your office?" Pat asked.

"Later, maybe. I just got a call that I need to respond to right away. We can talk later. I can meet you at the Centennial Golf Course if you know where it is." he paused for confirmation.

"Yes, I know where it is. I was just there," he said. Pat was surprised and pleased the Detective was taking him seriously enough to meet with him at the place the whole situation began.

"I'll see you there in half an hour. Don't make any stops on the way, Doctor."

Pat rushed to the elevator and downstairs to the valet stand in front of the Hilton where his rental car sat waiting. He pulled into light traffic and drove the twenty-minute route to the Centennial Golf Course in fifteen.

He saw the emergency lights flashing from some distance off, and when he pulled into the almost empty parking lot, he saw two ambulances and two Herndon Police patrol cars and a Chevy Impala with a flashing light on the dash.

As he approached the front, he was stopped by a yellow strip of crime scene tape and a police officer who instructed him to come back another time. Pat explained that he was supposed to meet Detective Saunders there. The police officer spoke into his shoulder mike, and a minute later a call came back to bring the Dr. to the lobby.

As Pat followed his escort into the lobby of the golf center, a body was being brought out on a gurney by two EMTs. As the body rolled by, Pat glanced down and saw the sun-weathered hand of Chain McLarney on the side of the gurney just outside the sheet that covered his lifeless body. He felt sick and was thankful he had not had time for breakfast before leaving the hotel.

A balding man of forty was walking out of the Pro Shop as Pat entered the lobby and thought about going left into the restroom to vomit, but his name was called out from his right.

"Dr. Rivera is it?" called the Detective. Pat looked in his direction, and at that moment, another gurney was being rolled out of the Pro Shop with another body under a sheet. Pat's heart sank as he thought about the sweet, young woman Carrie, who had made the mistake of helping him out of kindness and now may have been the victim of a homicide herself. Pat stopped and stared as the gurney rolled by, and a tear came unwelcomed to his right eye.

"Did you know these people, Dr. Rivera?" asked the Detective.

"I didn't know them really. I met Mr. McLarney a couple of days ago. 'Chain' was very helpful and seemed like such a nice old man. I only spoke with Carrie on the phone a couple of times. Didn't actually meet her when I was here," he said.

"Her? The second victim isn't a 'her'. It's a guy that worked as a Golf Pro here. Greg Landers. You know him?" pried the Detective.

"No. I never met him when I was here, and I'm not sure if he answered the phone when I called. Where is Carrie Darling? Has she been hurt? Is she okay?"

Pat looked around for any younger-looking woman that fit the mental image he had of the voice on the telephone. Seeing none, he returned his attention to the Detective.

"Why did you ask me to meet you here? Why did I need to see this. Detective?"

Saunders looked him over and said, "This is what Homicide looks like Dr. Rivera. In your profession, I'm sure you've seen people die before, but murder is different. It looks different. It feels different. And it is different. I'm guessing these two folks caught it by a professional killer,"

Saunders said and kept his eyes fixed on those of Dr. Rivera, looking for his reaction.

"A professional…you mean like a hitman? Like a mafia thing?" Pat sputtered as he neared hysteria.

"A pro for sure but not necessarily mob-related," Saunders said. "Whoever did the shooting used a silencer because nobody out here heard a thing, and these walls are not soundproof."

Pat was instantly sick and much more alarmed than he had been up until then. He excused himself and ran to the restroom where he dry-heaved a couple of times. He rinsed his face with cold water and stood looking in the mirror for a minute while he steadied his breathing and heartbeat. He returned to the lobby to find Detective Saunders waiting for him.

"You all right, Dr. Rivera? Maybe you don't see a lot of dead people in your practice," he said.

Pat decided it was time to clear up the confusion. "I'm a Ph.D.," he said. "Not a physician. I don't see death; I see viruses and bacterial strains under a microscope. I do research to find ways to kill pathogens and develop cures to make lives better or last longer. I don't see death," he repeated.

Detective Saunders listened to what Pat said and the way he said it, and his sense was that he was telling the truth, and he felt guilty for having exposed this innocent young man to the brutality of the scene, even though he had not allowed him into the Pro Shop and office where two lives were taken. Pat had remained in the lobby where the sight of brain matter and blood on the walls was not visible.

Saunders radio chirped on his belt, and he raised it to speak as he stepped away from Pat, who stood in the center of the lobby, just twenty feet from the counter where he had spoken to the weathered old man just two days earlier. He felt as though he needed to sit down to catch his breath again when the Detective returned to his side.

"There's somebody coming up from the tape. Wait here a minute." The Detective walked to the front and held open the door as a woman of about fifty stepped inside. Her hair was more grey than brown and pulled back plainly with a clip, and she was dressed in a white skirt and teal golf shirt with the Centennial logo on a patch on the left side. She held a pair of glasses in her hand and was openly crying, using the palm of her left hand to wipe mascara and tears from her face.

Detective Saunders walked her over to where Pat stood and introduced them to each other. Pat was genuinely surprised that Carrie was not in her late teens or early twenties based on the youthful sound of her voice on the telephone.

"Thank God you were not here. It looks like someone robbed the place, and some people got hurt," Pat said.

Carrie replied through sobs, "I know. They told me out front that Chain and Greg were hurt. It's all my fault," she blurted.

The Detective had started walking away but stopped and turned around upon hearing this. "How's that?" he asked. "How is any of this your fault?"

Carrie responded, "After I talked to you this morning," looking directly at Pat, "I called and asked Greg to set aside the tape so it wouldn't be written over. Greg came in earlier than usual to help me out. Otherwise, he would just now be showing up to open the Pro Shop. He wouldn't even have been here," she added.

Pat began to explain to the Detective all about the missing putter and the video tape from the parking lot camera that showed someone taking the putter after his cousin had passed away on the putting green.

The three of them walked together into a small lounge called The Nineteenth Green and sat at a table where Pat went on to explain everything that made him think there was more to this than simply a fatal heart attack. The Detective listened and wrote notes in a small stenographer's pad and asked a few questions along the way. When the conversation ended, Detective Saunders had made up his mind that he had three homicides to work, rather than two.

CHAPTER 5

"A lawsuit is the least of your worries," shouted Detective Saunders. He was sitting across a large mahogany desk from a very pale and hyperventilating Funeral Director for Manassas Funeral Services. "You may be looking at three to five years for destroying evidence in a homicide."

Despite his hopes of preventing it from happening, the body of Dr. Patrick Rivera had been cremated based on a written directive received by fax and signed by an attorney claiming to represent the Rivera family. The fax originated in Garland, Texas, and bore the signature of an attorney listed in Richardson, Texas, a city on the northeastern edge of Dallas proper.

It took one telephone call and two threats to determine that Attorney Ahn Zhi had retired several years earlier after suffering a stroke. There was no way he was still representing anyone in any legal matter. When practicing, his specialty had been Patents and Proprietary Law. He never worked in Family Law at all.

Detective Saunders got the fax the Funeral Director had received after allowing him to make a copy. He asked for and received the name of the Cremation Director at Jenkins Funeral Home, the actual site of the cremation.

Twenty minutes later, he showed his identification and was ushered into a large private office of Nathaniel Jenkins III, Director, as the gold stenciled nameplate read. Jenkins had the same authorization form faxed from Texas, claiming to be legal representation for the family of Dr. Patrick Rivera, along with a signed addendum to a Last Will and Testament of the deceased Dr. Rivera, which included an Advanced Directive to cremate. Everything appeared to them to be legal and above board.

A check of the originating fax number showed Detective Saunders that the big law firm in Richardson, Texas, was using a fax machine at a Kinko's store in a small strip center in Garland, Texas. Strange.

Saunders had been on the Centennial Triple homicide case for five days and had talked with Pat Rivera every day since taking it on. Rivera had returned to Dallas with his cousin's ashes in a cardboard container inside a sealed metal container included with his checked luggage on Monday, just six days after his death.

The entire family was devastated by the news of the cremation, which went against their wishes and those of their deceased loved one. Some members of the family wanted to file a lawsuit against the Jenkins Funeral Home, The Manassas County Coroner, and even the police department for the botched investigation, now that it was accepted that something other than a natural death probably took place.

The videotape that showed the collapse and death of Patrick was gone. Taken during the murder and burglary of Centennial the previous Saturday morning.

The only living witness that had seen the video was Carrie Darling, and Saunders had encouraged her to go visit a relative with a different last name in another state for her own protection. He couldn't adequately protect her if she stayed at home and continued working at the golf course. Centennial had not yet reopened but would soon, with Chain McLarney's son, David, taking over the operation.

Pat awoke early on Wednesday morning and telephoned Detective Saunders to ask about something he had thought about when sleep eluded him, which was most of the night. They had gotten to know and respect one another over the past week and had given up the Doctor and Detective monikers for first names only.

"Morning, Gary. I hope I'm not calling too early."

It was a quarter past seven on the east coast and six fifteen in Dallas. "Nope. I've been up a while. Taking my son to school on the way to the office. What's up?"

"I had a thought and wanted to run it past you," Pat said.

"Shoot," Saunders replied as he poured coffee into a thermos.

"Were all the videotapes missing, or just the one for the day Patrick was killed?"

"There were five taken from the shelf and the one that was in the VHS player, so six in all," he recalled. "Why are you asking?"

"Well, the killer somehow knew we were looking at the video, and it was important enough to kill for. That means he was either listening to my calls somehow or following me wherever I went," Pat said. "I mean, if he's a pro, as you said, I guess he could just be covering his bases and just went back to see if video evidence was there. But it seems strange."

"Yeah, I suppose it does. So where are you going with this?"

"If there are any tapes left behind, maybe there's one that shows when I went there on Thursday, and maybe the killer followed me there that day too. Carrie said the car that picked up the putter was a light-colored vehicle, right?" he said.

"Yeah, she did. We showed her a vehicle photo lineup with several cars and narrowed it down to either a Toyota Four Runner or a Mercedes SUV. Either silver or white."

"I'll stop by Centennial this morning and check it out," and then the call ended so Saunders could start his busy day of trying to solve a triple homicide.

Having struck out at Centennial because the only remaining videotape was from the prior Sunday, Saunders expounded on the idea Pat had shared with him. He had to have been followed unless someone had tapped into the telephone lines at the Hilton, which was where Pat had made all his calls and received his messages.

He stopped at the Hilton Hotel in Reston and spoke with the General Manager, who allowed him access to the telephone control room to see if there were any wiretaps or other anomalies with the equipment, but there were none.

He then asked about security video in or around the property and was told they had several cameras on each level of the parking deck, two on the entrance at both ends of the portico, six additional cameras around the exterior, and more than forty cameras inside the hotel. Saunders felt like he had struck gold!

The cameras were the latest in surveillance technology, and whatever they captured was digitized in a daily backup process so the same microtapes could be used repeatedly without losing valuable information. The digital backups were stored on a server with redundancy at their corporate headquarters in Richmond.

Saunders placed a call to the main office of the Parker Group, the franchise owner of the Hilton, and spoke with the Director of Hotel Security. Ken Vogel was a retired Richmond PD detective, and after Saunders explained what he was looking for and that it didn't involve any other guests or hotel employees, Vogel agreed to let Saunders look at the video archives for the Reston property.

Saunders made the two-and-half-hour drive south to Richmond and was met in the lobby by a wiry man in his mid-fifties that was obviously making a better income in the private sector than he ever did as a cop.

Vogel was wearing an expensive shirt and tie with leather suspenders that matched his Italian loafers and no jacket when he greeted Saunders in the lobby. Gold cufflinks and a gold Tag Heuer watch completed the look of the new success he presented. A guest badge was provided to allow him entry, and Saunders was asked to sign a registry to chronicle his visit.

Vogel led Saunders to the elevator and up one floor to the Security Office and showed him to a cubicle where he could view the recordings. Pat had stayed at the Reston Hilton from Wednesday until the following Monday when he returned to Dallas. Saunders began at the beginning.

Wednesday evening, between nine and nine-thirty, when Pat Rivera first arrived in a blue Toyota Camry. It took ten minutes at double the normal speed to see a blue Camry pull under the Hilton portico. Saunders hit the button to slow the viewing speed.

He was watching a split screen so he could see the front of the car on the right side of the monitor and the rear of the car on the left side. As he watched, Pat handed a key to the valet attendant through the open driver's side window, stepped out of the car, retrieved a large rolling suitcase from the trunk, put the strap of a carry-on bag over his shoulder, then walked into the hotel.

He continued watching the video for the next sixty minutes of recording time to see if a light-colored SUV had appeared. His hopes were raised when a white Mercedes pulled in almost thirty minutes after Pat, and then they were dashed when a woman and two children climbed out.

The woman then retrieved a third child from a car seat in the back on the passenger side of the car, placed the sleeping child in a stroller, and walked inside. After an hour of watching the portico camera recordings on the days and times Pat was there and coming or going, Saunders decided the answer wasn't there.

He remembered something Pat had told him and checked his stenographer's notepad for the details. He then pulled up the recording for the pool area on one side of the monitor and the lobby on the other, for Friday, around two in the afternoon. He watched as Pat entered around twenty past two. He looked around and then stepped into a wooden door marked Sauna – Adult Guests Only.

Saunders watched carefully for anyone else to enter, but nobody did. At the two forty-one-mark, Pat stepped out of the sauna, laid a towel on a chair poolside, and stepped off into the swimming pool. He spent the next fifteen minutes swimming up and back in full view of the camera, then climbed out on the side of the pool. He picked up his towel and started toweling off when he suddenly stopped and looked in the direction of the camera as though someone had entered the pool area.

Saunders looked on the lobby camera feed and could see the shoulder and leg of someone standing in the doorway of the swimming pool entry. On the other screen, Pat was looking over his shoulder behind himself and then back to the door. He shrugged and continued drying off.

Pat watched as an Asian man walked hurriedly across the lobby, out the door, and toward the parking lot. He loaded the video file for the north parking lot and saw the man climb into a silver Infinity SUV with another man in the passenger seat. They talked briefly, and then the vehicle started, backed out of the parking space, and left through the eastern exit of the lot.

As the SUV turned, a partial plate became visible, as well as a parking decal on the passenger side of the front windshield. Pat wasn't sure how to zoom in to see it more clearly, so he paused the feed and sought out Vogel, who was in his office on a call. Vogel held up a finger indicating Saunders should hold a second while he finished his call.

"Polygraph the Bartender and the Room Service Head Server and let me know. One of them is lying, and it will be the one that refuses to take it."

He listened for a few seconds and said, "Okay. Do that, and I'll talk to you after. Thanks, Leon," and then he hung up the phone.

"You get what you needed, Detective?" Vogel asked.

"I'm close. I got a vehicle with a parking permit and a partial plate. I need to get a closer look at the decal. Can you help me out?" he asked.

They walked back to the visitor's cubical, and Vogel used the mouse to click a pulldown menu and select a screen change from normal to five hundred percent, and the windshield of the car filled the screen. The decal blurred considerably, and Saunders leaned in to try to make out what it said.

"Can you clear that up," Sloane asked.

"Maybe a little," and Vogel adjusted the screen zoom to reduce it to fifty percent. The decal was off the screen, so Vogel shifted things around with the mouse pointer, and the decal slid into view. It was Dark blue and silver, and Saunders could read the name clearly. Global Achievements.

"Can I get a copy of this?" Sloan asked hopefully.

"That I cannot do. Not without a warrant. But I will archive this file so when you come back with a warrant, it will be ready for you."

"Fair enough. If I send you the warrant, can you email the file?"

"I'm afraid it's too big to go as an attachment. You'll have to pick it up on a DVD in person. Chain of evidence rules and all that." Vogel said.

"I'll be back tomorrow. This may break three homicides for me, so don't lose that file," Sloan said and shook Vogel's hand. "I really appreciate this, brother."

Vogel liked helping out brothers in blue more than anything else. "Not even a little sweat Saunders. Happy to help. Especially if it takes a triple off the street."

He walked Saunders to the elevator and then to the front door of the Parker Group offices. Saunders left the Richmond area on I-95, headed back to Herndon. The two-hour drive would give him plenty of windshield time – time to think and put some of the puzzle pieces together so he could make sense of his investigation.

He thought, *I've got a doctor from Dallas attending a three-day conference at Global Achievements. He blows off all but the first day and hits the links, only to die of what? A freaking heart attack at thirty-two years old? I've got another doctor from Dallas who starts turning over stones, and everybody he talks to starts dropping.*

His low fuel light came on, and an annoying ding-ding started chiming every thirty seconds.

"Okay, okay. I'll get gas. Enough is enough already," he said as if the car could understand him. He saw a sign for an AMOCO station ahead at the exit for a racetrack, signaled, and took the off-ramp.

He pulled to a stop sign and thought that while he was at the gas station, he should use the payphone to call his wife and let her know he'd be eating dinner at the office tonight. Not an unusual event in his life or marriage. His job was not a nine-to-five.

He was just getting ready to turn right to drive to the gas station when a vehicle pulled beside him in the left turn lane. He glanced to his left and just had enough time for his eyes to register what was happening before his head exploded. The two shots fired from the silenced forty-caliber handgun hit their mark, and Detective Sloan and his investigation were both dead. A small object was tossed through the shattered driver-side window.

The black sedan turned left, and Sloan's car drifted slowly to the right and came to a stop with the left wheel up on the median strip and the front bumper wedged against an Interstate sign that read I-95 N with a right arrow and Reston eighty-seven miles.

The incendiary device went off, and a fireball erupted inside the car and blew the windows and the sunroof out. Flames shot out in all directions as the phosphorus ignited, bringing the inferno instantly to over fifteen hundred degrees, and the fire spread sixty feet in every direction. The fire department vehicles that arrived four minutes later could only stand and watch the fire burn itself out, as their foam and water proved to be useless in extinguishing the flames.

## CHAPTER 6

Research Lead Dr. Pat Rivera sat at a lab table in Richardson, Texas, looking through an electron microscope at stem cells on a slide and making notes on a Toshiba laptop. The twelfth floor of Tower Three was the principal location for the most significant research and development Warner was conducting.

Warner Pharmaceuticals was one of the largest employers in the state and a producer of some of the best, most effective medicines on the American market. A perennial name on the Forbes One Hundred and a stock that Montgomery Street and Wall Street loved.

Their operations in Mexico and Canada enabled them to dominate the market in North America for the top cancer treatments available, and they were the first to develop an effective treatment for HIV. The disease, which many in the Bible belt referred to as the "gay virus," had, in fact, attacked indiscriminately due to how it spread through blood transfusions and weak control protocols in the national blood bank network.

Pat was leading a team working on blood testing protocols, developing a way to improve the long-term prognosis for both cancer and AIDS victims using embryonic stem cells. It was controversial, and picket signs and protesters were common in front of the Warner Tower in Richardson. He also had another team working on new prophylactics for Type Two diabetes and safe, controlled weight loss for morbidly obese patients.

He never saw picket signs protesting weight loss. Pat stopped at lunchtime and made a call to the Herndon, Virginia, Police Department and asked to speak with Detective Saunders. After being placed on hold for a couple of minutes, the same person came back on the line and identified himself.

"This is Sergeant Duckworth. Who should I say is calling?" he asked.

"Pat Rivera. Dr. Pat Rivera," he replied and was placed on hold again. He waited for over three minutes and was about to hang up and call again when the line was picked up.

"Lieutenant Morrissey here. You're calling for Detective Saunders?" he asked.

Getting a little exasperated by how many people he had to talk to just to get through to Gary, Pat said, "Yes, and I've been waiting for over five minutes. If he's busy, I'd be happy to call back later."

"Can I ask what this is about?" asked the lieutenant.

"The detective is working on my cousin's case. He was murdered two weeks ago at one of your golf courses, and I'm just trying to get an update if he's available," Pat said, trying hard to keep the edge out of his voice.

"Detective Saunders is unavailable. He, uh, he isn't working on that case anymore. It's been reassigned," the lieutenant started, and Pat lost a little bit of control.

"Reassigned? What the hell? He knows everything about my case!" Pat shouted.

"Rivera, listen to me. Another detective has taken over Saunders's cases because he is, he ah, he can't work them himself. What case is it he was working for you? I know, the double homicide at the Centennial. Who was your cousin?" he asked, and Pat could hear papers shuffling.

"My cousin was Dr. Patrick Rivera. Same as my name before you get all tripped up. He was murdered at the Centennial."

"I've got two names of victims here, and neither one was a Dr. or named Rivera," he said. "You want to try again? I frankly don't have the time or the patience for this right now."

"Please put Gary on the phone," Pat implored. "He knows everything. I've been talking to him almost daily since this all began," he added.

Quietly, calmly, almost dejectedly, the lieutenant said, "He's dead. Gary's dead, Dr. Rivera. He was killed down by Richmond two days ago."

Panic and despair overcame Pat. "How did he die?" he asked solemnly.

"We don't have the full report back from Richmond PD yet, and I can't discuss details with you. I don't even know why he went to Richmond. Do you?"

"No. I have no idea. The last time I spoke to him, he was going back over to Centennial to look for a video. That was two days ago. He didn't say anything about going out of town. He was dropping his son off at school and…" Pat was on the verge of tears again, thinking about Gary's family. "I can't believe this has happened."

"Leave your contact information with me, and I'll make sure someone follows up with you when we know more," Morrissey said.

Morrissey wrote everything down as Pat dictated it and then said, "We'll be in touch, but it's going to take a while under the circumstances."

"I'm sorry. What circumstances?"

"Can't say. We'll be in touch," and the line disconnected.

Pat sat there and stared out the window at the road construction taking place beneath his window. He was heartbroken and scared. He was twenty-seven years old, and until two weeks earlier, he had only known one human being personally who had died other than elderly relatives.

Now, in the span of two weeks, he has personally known or been in contact with four people who have been killed. He didn't yet know the circumstances of Gary Saunders's death, but he knew it was not natural, and his gut told him it was connected to his cousin's investigation.

Two weeks went by, and Pat heard nothing from whoever had taken over the case in Herndon. One afternoon when he had submitted some reports ahead of schedule, with some extra time on his hands, he decided to make the call himself. He called the number he had committed to memory and was eventually connected to Detective Lisa Williams, a nineteen-year veteran now responsible for the late Gary Saunders's active cases.

"Homicide, Williams," she answered and sounded a bit rushed.

"Detective Williams, hi, this is Pat Rivera calling from Richardson, Texas, regarding the investigation of my cousin's murder. Gary Saunders was working the case before his, um, death," Pat managed to get it all out before the detective responded.

"Mr. Rivera, the case you are referring to is not a part of my caseload. It's not my case, or anyone's case because the Medical Examiner ruled your cousin's passing a natural death by a heart attack. That designation has not changed, and therefore, his death is not being investigated," she said firmly and a little coldly, and it was intentional.

She had to get this relative to stop calling the department and taking up valuable resources and time, especially her own. Her caseload of legitimate cases had doubled when Saunders' cases were assigned to her, and she had picked up another murder case that stemmed from a domestic violence situation. She had to get her ducks in a row for the District Attorney to present his case to a Grand Jury. She had no time to waste.

Pat was incensed by the dismissal and felt like he had lost a lot of ground. "What about the putter? What about the video? How can…"

"I have no idea what you are referring to, Mr. Rivera," she said.

"It was all in Gary Saunders's notes! We went over these points, and he agreed there was a case. He called it his triple murder case. I don't understand," Pat was almost pleading.

"All of Detective Saunders's notes were cremated with him," she blurted.

"Cremated? I'm sorry. Why would his notes…"

"The notes and everything he had on this case were in his car, and it burned to ash along with him after the incident," she explained. "I know you were waiting for us to call, but I honestly did not feel the need to update you on an active case and didn't feel it was my place to share what happened to Gary."

There was a long pause while this sank into Pat's head. "The fact of the matter is just as I said before. There is no case. I'm not working on your cousin's heart attack, and there is nothing else I can share with you," she concluded. She didn't ask if there was anything else she could do for him. She just said goodbye, and the line went to a dial tone on Pat's end.

## CHAPTER 7

Reston, Virginia - May 27, 1996

The office of Senator John Chapman was located in the Hart Senate Office Building, one of three buildings that housed the one hundred United States Senators, as well as non-voting shadow Senators from the District of Columbia, and one for the Vice President of the United States who resides as the President of the Senate.

Senator Chapman, from the Commonwealth of Virginia, was serving his fifth term in office, having been a fixture in Washington, D.C., for more than thirty years in the Senate and twelve years in Congress before that. He was currently the Minority Leader, as the Republicans had taken control in the House and Senate in the midterms. He spent most days in lengthy sessions of the Foreign Relations, Judicial, and Intelligence Committees, and on weekends, he made the rounds of the talk show circuit.

His patronage of Global Achievements opened no more doors than he already had access to, but the funding it generated for him and his party leadership seemed like an unending supply. The program Global Achievements first invited him to join in February. The GAP Council, Global Achievements PoliMed Council, promised to introduce him to some very powerful and interesting people.

His planned trip to China in late January had taken an interesting turn, transitioning from a planned tour of an auto factory and discussing the development of a logistics enterprise on mainland China turned into two days of in-depth discussions with two pharmaceutical giants about establishing a presence in America.

He visited a lab in Wuhan, China, and met with Dr. Leo Faucette, Director of the National Institute of Allergy and Infectious Diseases. Dr. Faucette had been introduced by Dr. Foster and seemed to have a very close relationship with the key speaker from the first day of the conference. Faucette was the highest-paid member of the GAP Team for Global Achievements and was the primary architect of the new initiative to be discussed when the meeting launched in May.

Senator Chapman was a scheduled speaker on the second day of the meeting and was scheduled to speak on the third day as well, according to the itinerary, but everything changed, and he had to excuse himself on day two to leave for China. Senator Chapman had been handed a note on the evening of the first day that simply said *leak*, and he stepped out to meet with his senior aide, Bart Kroonenberg, who waited in the lobby of the Global Achievements building.

"What the hell is that supposed to mean?" he asked curtly. He hated to be pulled out of a meeting, or in this case, away from the dinner table with the executive leadership present. It was going on eight pm, and they were still discussing the initiative that everyone present believed would save the American economy if they succeeded.

"There's a guy in town that attended the meeting today, and he's talking about it," the aide reported. "I know how hush-hush this meeting is supposed to be and thought you should know since you told me to never mention your association with, well with any of this."

"Who's the leak, and how do you know he's talking?" asked the Senator.

"I got a call from a friend who was setting up a golf outing tomorrow morning at The Centennial Golf Course. He got a call from this doctor friend that was here at the conference today. A doctor named Rivera. This Rivera told my buddy about attending a weird meeting and told him he'd tell him all about it while they played golf tomorrow. I just thought you should know," informed the aide.

The Senator stood there for a moment thinking and then asked, "How much does your friend know?"

"Nothing. Absolutely zip, Senator. He only knew that this Rivera had attended a meeting that was over his head and not the least bit interesting and that the guy wanted to play golf with his college buddy. My buddy asked if he could add a couple of guys to make it a foursome because the Golf Course has a rule, so he called me and another guy. That's it, Senator. What should I do?"

"Cancel it. Call the two people you know and cancel it. Tell them you got a call from Rivera, and he decided to go to the meeting instead. Don't mention where the meeting is or anything else. Do you understand?"

"Yes, sir. I got it," he said.

"Okay. Thank you for bringing this to me, Bartholomew." The Senator used his full name at times; he was most pleased with him. It was the same thing his dad and grandfather had done. Bart smiled and left to carry out his orders.

Senator Chapman went back into the private dining room and took his place at the table. He leaned over to Dr. Tau and said, "We have a problem."

He explained the situation, and Tau, who was no more a doctor than the Senator's aide was but used the title to sit in the meetings. His actual function was Head of Security for Global Achievements. Grant Hofstetter was at the table and heard part of the exchange. The Senator's voice tended to carry even when he was trying to be discreet.

"What kind of problem, Senator?" Hofstetter asked.

Tau responded, "A problem today but not so tomorrow."

Tau excused himself from the table and left the room. He went to his office on a lower level and looked up the information he needed for the little problem he had to deal with. He rode the elevator up to the sixth floor to a small dispensary, where he picked up a small spray bottle wrapped in plastic-lined foil.

The next morning Tau and his Security Chief drove to the Marriott hotel, where Dr. Rivera's schedule said he was staying while in Virginia. Tau sat on a sofa in the lobby reading the USA Today until Dr. Patrick Rivera exited the elevator carrying a Calloway golf bag. He crossed the lobby and went into a small breakfast room where a few guests were seated, and a spread of food, coffee, and juice was displayed at the far end of the room.

Dr. Rivera leaned his golf bag against the wall just inside the entrance to the room and walked over to the food table. Tau slipped a bottle from his pocket and sprayed the grip of the putter. He then unzipped the pocket holding a dozen or more golf balls and sprayed them generously with a lethal dose of botulinum toxin he had formulated in the small lab at Global Achievements dispensary.

The deadly toxin had been provided by Dr. Hofstetter from the labs of the World Health Organization for just such situations. Tau had used this method of removing problems before when circumstances required discretion, and it was always successful.

As he turned to walk away, Dr. Rivera turned from the food table and recognized him. They spoke briefly, and Tau left, leaving Rivera with the idea that Tau was also staying at the hotel.

Within forty minutes, Dr. Patrick Rivera would be dead of an apparent heart attack.

CHAPTER 8

Bart had received a call after eleven that same night from the Senator, wanting to confirm the situation with the golfers had been handled. During this call, the Senator said he had a car coming to pick him up, and he should bring his passport; he would explain more when he arrived. The car arrived ten minutes later, and Bart rushed out, sensing the urgency in the Senator's voice.

The car took Bart, surprisingly, to Senator Chapman's residence in Georgetown, where the Senator was waiting to speak to him. The Senator invited Bart into his library with floor-to-ceiling bookshelves filled with leather-bound tomes, law books, and a collection of classics.

The room smelled faintly of cigar smoke, and the thick carpeting made the room feel warm and very quiet. The Senator's deep voice seemed even lower than usual as he asked Bart a number of questions, including the names of the friends he had called to cancel the golf game.

Bart had respectfully asked the Senator why it was necessary to provide that since they didn't know anything at all about the Senator's business affairs.

Chapman had said, "Fair enough, Bartholomew. I think you know that this one is critical to my interests, both in Washington, D.C. and in Virginia, but if you are convinced these friends of yours are not a threat to those interests, that's good enough for me."

The Senator stood up from an overstuffed leather wing chair with a slight grunt and walked to a Bart, offered Bart a drink which he declined, refilled his own, and then said, "I want you to accompany me on this trip, Bart."

Bart was surprised because he knew the Senator's schedule, and the only trip he had planned was to China later in the week.

"To China, sir?"

"Yes, of course, to China. I have some high-level meetings planned, and you will be a big help to me."

At seventy-seven years old, the Senator still maintained a very heavy work and travel schedule, but it surprised Bart when he said, "We will leave for Dulles in ten minutes. You brought your passport as I instructed?"

Bart had, and they left for the airport but first drove to the Hart Senate Office Building, where Senator Chapman picked up some documents while Bart waited in the car with the driver, an Asian man who did not speak a word the entire trip. He just looked at Bart in the rearview mirror a lot.

The flight out of Dulles International Airport to Beijing took a little over twenty-seven hours, with a brief stop and change of aircraft in Honolulu, Hawaii. It was the first international trip the Senator had allowed Bart Kroonenberg to accompany him on. The Senator was four rows in front of Bart on the United flight, in the last row of first-class seats.

The Senator read or slept, and they did not speak at all while en route but spoke briefly in the American Airlines Admirals Club, to which the Senator had a Platinum Membership. They had a cocktail, and Senator Chapman instructed Bart on a few things he needed to know.

"When we get to Beijing, you will be assigned a guide. This person will serve as an interpreter unless you are fluent in Mandarin," the Senator said and raised an eyebrow as though he were really asking.

"No, sir. A little Spanish, but."

The Senator waved him off and continued speaking, "Rhetorical son. I would know if you could speak pig Latin, let alone Chinese. Anyway. This guide and interpreter is a handler for the state. Under no circumstances are you to go anywhere or talk to anyone without this person being present. Do you understand?" he asked.

"Understood." Bart nervously replied.

"This trip is going to go really fast with the meetings I have lined up, and I won't need you to be in all of them, so your guide can show you around. Just go with it and enjoy the ride, son."

"Yes, sir. Like a tourist, sir," Bart said. He was so proud to have been included on this trip at the last minute. He didn't even have time to call his family, and the Senator asked for his utmost discretion, and of course, he complied. Bart had not had time to pack a bag, but the Senator said he could pick up everything he needed once they landed in Beijing. Having heard the last statement, Bart wondered why he had been invited at all.

"And most important of all Bartholomew, these friends of yours. The golfing friends you spoke with. When we get back to Virginia, you must cut off all communications with them. They no longer are a part of your life," the Senator stated and looked directly at Bart, who was just about to sip his cocktail and stopped short of his lips, and Chapman, having Bart's full attention, confirmed, "Is that also understood?"

It was, and Bart said so, despite the chill that ran down his back at the icy glare the Senator was giving him. For the first time since Bart had been working for the Senator, he found himself on the receiving end of the look that made junior and tenured Senators cave to his will. The look that he gave lobbyists who gave more and more to his coffers to sway his opinion on matters from gun control to mineral rights. A whole host of legislation landed on Bart's desk for review before passing it on to Senator Chapman with notes, highlights, arrows, and tabs.

The flight to Beijing was called over the loudspeaker in the Admirals Club lounge, and Senator Chapman boarded with the first group who moved to the upper level of the aircraft, and twenty minutes later, Bart squeezed into a middle seat in the center section of coach. He didn't mind the cramped accommodations because he was excited to have become a part of Senator Chapman's inner circle of confidants. It was a heady feeling for him as a twenty-nine-year-old graduate of George Mason University's Schar School of Policy and Government. He never imagined a young black man could rise so quickly in Washington, D.C., and all it took was listening and absorbing all he could from the power brokers that surrounded him daily.

On the Lufthansa flight from Honolulu to Beijing, they were separated by a greater distance as First Class was on the upper level near the lounge on the Airbus 380. Bart asked for a pillow and blanket just after the fasten seat belt sign was turned off by the pilot and the safety announcements concluded. He put on headphones connected to his new mp3 player and soon dozed off, listening to Kenny G playing softly in his ears.

The overnight flight landed in Beijing at just past eleven am Eastern Time, but just after six in the evening local time the next day. The flight crossed the international date line somewhere over the Pacific, causing them to lose a day that they would recapture on the return flight.

The flight arrived without a hitch, except for a crying toddler whose favorite word was "no!" that managed to infiltrate Bart's noise-canceling headphones despite the best efforts of Kenny G and Natalie Merchant. Bart exited the aircraft and made his way up the ramp to the terminal.

He stepped through the doorway to find the busiest airport he had ever seen, with literally thousands of people walking the causeway and filling the many gates nearby. He stepped to the side of a red velvet rope and waited to see the Senator come up the ramp, but after twenty minutes, the plane was empty, and Senator Chapman was nowhere in sight.

A young man in a black suit, holding a sign at his side, spoke loudly and in broken English asked, "Mr. Kroonenberg?"

Startled and still confused at not seeing the Senator disembark, Bart turned to face the young man, who appeared to be a little younger than himself.

"That's me. I'm Mr., or I mean, I'm Bart Kroonenberg," he stammered.

"Please follow me. I take you to the hotel now," he raised his right arm to show Bart the way.

An announcement was being made over the loudspeaker in Mandarin, followed by French, and finally in English. Bart listened as the recorded voice instructed all international passengers to go to the nearest Customs Enforcement Area.

Bart said, "I need a minute. I'm waiting for Senator Chapman to join me, then we can leave."

"He gone. We go," the man with the sign said and again raised his arm to show the way out.

Bart was unsure of what to do. He was fiercely loyal to the Senator, but he had been told to listen and obey his guide while in Beijing.

"I need to make sure the Senator is okay and on time. Please, can we wait a few more minutes?"

Frustrated and feeling like he was not being understood, the man with the sign said, "John Chapman, leave with driver. We go. Have long way."

They walked toward the Customs Enforcement counter, and an armed officer looked at the young man and simply nodded for him and Bart to go through. Reluctantly and feeling like a foreign fish out of the water, Bart followed the young man at a hurried pace down the causeway. They stepped onto a wide conveyor belt and continued to walk at a fast pace, which made Bart feel like he was sprinting.

They exited the Lufthansa Terminal and walked across eight lanes of traffic to a parking garage where a grey Hong Qi sedan was parked. Bart started to get into the front passenger seat, but the young man, who had not provided a name yet, placed a hand on his arm and said, "You sit back," and he opened the back door for Bart.

As they drove out of the parking garage and merged into incredibly heavy traffic, Bart said, "My name is Bart. What is your name?"

The driver looked at him in the rearview mirror but said nothing.

"I guess we will be spending a lot of time together over the next couple of days, so it will be easier if we know each other's names, don't you think?"

That got another quick glance in the mirror, but no words were spoken, and no names were exchanged. Bart sat back in his leather seat, fastened his seat belt, and looked out the window at the traffic and the low-hanging, yellow smog of car fumes and factory exhausts that obscured the view of the Beijing skyline.

Bart rode in silence for over an hour through heavy traffic until they were driving around a beautifully landscaped park. There were dozens of couples walking together on a paved footpath, and a small group of elderly people were practicing Tai Chi and Wu Shu with bamboo swords.

It made Bart recall growing up in Chesterfield, a suburb of Philadelphia, Pennsylvania. He had been adopted as a baby. His adoptive parents were a successful physician father and a loving and attentive mother. His upbringing was far from common for a young black child whose birth mother, he later discovered, had given him up for a better life than she could afford to give him.

His adoptive parents made sure he had the best of everything, whether it was clothing, education, religion, or sports and extracurricular activities, but most importantly, the love of two devoted parents. Ira and Sophia Kroonenberg made him the man worthy of the trust of a United States Senator.

Bart had started taking martial arts at the age of six and achieved a black belt by the time he started middle school. His parents were almost as serious about his self-defense classes as they were about his learning the Torah.

His mother used to tell him, "Do everything you do with full commitment, and your life will always be full."

Bart's mother was an expert in Krav Maga, an Israeli form of martial arts. Her gentleness as a mother did not extend to the training sessions and exercise regimen Bart initially suffered through and eventually flourished in.

His training as a fighter never became useful to him growing up because his father also taught him how to avoid physical injury through observation, negotiation, and awareness of his surroundings. He was very popular in school and was known to be studious and friendly to everyone who met or taught him.

Bart watched couples practicing ballroom dancing on a tennis court they used as a dance floor in the park as the luxury sedan drove slowly through the park. Bart could see a large sign glowing over the treetops that read Lijingwan International Hotel. A minute later, they pulled under a glass and steel portico, and the car came to a stop.

The driver remained seated as a valet opened the door for Bart to exit. Bart remained seated and asked the driver if he was supposed to follow him or go inside. The driver responded without so much as a glance in the rearview mirror, "You go Sōngsǎn de yīduān."

That was the first time Bart heard his name spoken in a foreign language. He possessed a keen ear for dialect, and in his mind, he repeated the name "Sōngsǎn de yīduān" several times, committing it to memory.

Checking into the Lijingwan International Hotel was as simple as showing his passport and credit card to the front desk clerk, who assigned Bart a room on the eleventh floor and informed him his room was taken care of by the Chapman party. A button was pressed, and a melodic chime played for a moment as a Bellman appeared and looked confused at finding no luggage to carry.

The room key was handed to the Bellman, and a portfolio to Bart, and he followed the Bellman to a bank of elevators. They walked past a ballroom replete with massive crystal chandeliers where a wedding party was celebrating. He looked into a darkened lounge that was full of smoke and people drinking with a couple on a small stage singing a song in Mandarin.

They stepped onto the elevator with two couples who pressed the fourth-floor button and asked in English, to Bart's surprise, "What floor?" to which the Bellman said "one, one," and the polished brass doors closed.

The ride to the fourth floor was quick, and Bart could feel his stomach fill with butterflies and realized he hadn't eaten anything since the first leg of the flight. He had managed to sleep through food service on the flight from Honolulu to Beijing and made up his mind to order room service as soon as he got to his room.

The room was extraordinarily beautiful, with a king-sized bed and a sofa with two side chairs. A desk and leather chair set against the far wall with a large television cabinet whose doors were slid open to reveal a television and music console.

A bottle of water in a champagne bucket with melting ice sat on a mirrored tray on a credenza, with a small pool of condensation encircling the bucket. Bart opened the one-and-a-half-liter bottle of Nongfu Spring water and poured himself a glass. He took a long drink and walked to the window.

Opening the heavy curtains with a pull rod revealed a beautiful view of the park below and the city skyscape beyond the bucolic scene below, in the midst of one of the largest metropolitan areas on earth.

The part of Beijing visible through the yellowish haze of the smog was beautiful as the sun was beginning to set and lights were coming on all over the bustling metropolis. A knock at the door interrupted Bart's visual tour of the park from one hundred forty feet above it.

A young female whose Lijingwan International Hotel name tag said she was Lǐ Yún stood at the door holding two shopping bags with the hotel's name emblazoned on the side.

"Hello," Bart said, admiring the beauty of the Chinese woman standing at his door.

With a little dialectic difficulty, the woman said, "Good evening, Mr. Kroonenberg," and it sounded like crooning bug, which made Bart smile. Trying to impress her with his ability to pick up the local language, Bart replied,

"Please call me, Sōngsǎn de yīduān."

To this, the woman looked confused but returned Bart's warm smile and said, "I have your clothes and personal items," and she lifted the bags to him. Bart reached out to take the bags, and she said, "No. I put up for you," and she entered the room.

Bart watched as she pulled articles of clothing from the bags and hung up two white shirts and placed a package of boxer underwear in a drawer, along with two pairs of dark socks and two silk ties. She carried a bag of toiletries into the bathroom and set them out on the marble countertop. Returning to the main room, she asked. "Is there more you need now?" and smiled brightly.

"No ma'am. I can't believe you brought all of this! My sizes too. Thank you very much, Miss Yún," Bart said.

"Miss Lǐ" she corrected, "Yún first name. Lǐ second," she added.

"Why you are name Sōngsǎn de yīduān?" she asked.

"My driver from the airport called me that, and I memorized it. I thought it would be cool to be able to introduce myself in Mandarin. Does it mean Bart Kroonenberg?" he asked.

She smiled and said slowly, "No. Bart Kroonenberg means Bart Kroonenberg," and it still sounded like Bar Crooning Bug when she said it, and Bart smiled widely.

"Sōngsǎn de yīduān mean loose end," and the smile faded from Bart's lips.

CHAPTER 9

Bart was starting to put two and two together, and it was adding up to trouble for Arthur Kroonenberg's adopted son. He thought back to the icy stare the Senator had given him and even further back to the conversation when he told him about the telephone call with the doctor he was to golf with on Tuesday.

The Senator had told him to cancel and to let his two buddies know the game was canceled by Rivera. He had done exactly what was asked of him, and the next thing he knew, the Senator had invited him on a rushed trip to China. But how could he be of any help to the Senator if he was never intended to be a part of the meetings, he wondered.

Bart felt as though the walls of the beautiful hotel suite were closing in on him, and he had to do something before it was too late. Bart was feeling very uncomfortable with his situation and decided he should call his father to let him know where he was.

He lifted the phone, and a voice spoke English to him, asking for the number. When Bart provided the telephone number in Philadelphia, USA, the voice said, "I'm sorry, sir. Your phone is restricted to local calls only."

His situation was getting more bleak by the moment. He changed into one of the new shirts delivered by the young woman from the boutique in the lobby, took his passport out of his suit coat, and left the room after hanging a "do not disturb" sign on the door. He made sure every light in the room was on, and the blackout curtains were completely open.

Using the stairs instead of the glass bubble the hotel used for elevator cars, Bart went to the lobby and down a long hallway to the attached parking garage. He walked down the ramp to the exit that faced the expansive park and walked quickly across to a bench near a copse of trees and a jogging trail.

He took a seat on the bench with his back to the hotel, a little over eighty yards behind him, and turned so he could see the rooms, and after a few seconds, he found his room on the eleventh floor.

He sat and intermittently watched his room and the tennis court, which was brightly lit and had several couples dancing to big band music from the US.

Bart had been sitting there for almost two hours and had started feeling like he was paranoid when something caught his eye on the eleventh floor. The lighting changed, and suddenly a figure was standing in his window, and then the curtains were drawn. The "Do Not Disturb" door hanger would have prevented hotel staff from entering his room, so whoever was in his room was uninvited and not up to anything good.

Bart rose and walked across the park and out of view of anyone at the hotel and started trying to come up with a way to get back home. He walked out of the park after walking a mile or more and continued along the road he had been driven on three hours earlier. Bart stepped into a bank lobby with an exchange ATM kiosk and converted three hundred American dollars for yuan notes. He came to a row of restaurants and Barts and thought about food for the first time since leaving Washington DC.

He motioned to the hostess who greeted him that he wanted a table in the back where he sat facing the door and looked at everyone in the little restaurant and anyone who came in to see if they paid any attention to him at all. Fortunately, nobody seemed to notice him or pay any special interest to what he was doing.

He used cash to check into a hostel that was unlike anything he had ever seen. It was essentially a bed in a room with five other beds set up in two stacks of three. There were two Asian men in the room when he entered, and he chose an upper bunk across the room from them. Nobody talked at all until Bart sat up to climb down to go to the restroom and hit his head on a light sconce.

"Ow, damn it!" he blurted and then hopped down to the floor.

"American?" the man on the bottom bunk across the room asked.

Bart looked over in surprise to hear his native language and said, "Canadian" Bart lied. He walked into the bathroom and returned a couple of minutes later and climbed the ladder at the end of his bunk stack and climbed under the blanket. He shut off the light, and the man across the room asked, "Toronto?"

"Excuse me?" Bart replied.

"Are you from Toronto? I spent time in Toronto after college. Lovely area," the stranger said.

"British Columbia. The other end of the road," Bart said and turned towards the wall to sleep.

The next morning when Bart awoke to the sound of buzzing coming from the open bathroom door, he rose and slipped down to the floor. He had no toiletries with him, so he pulled his new shirt off the back of the chair, put it on, and slipped into his shoes.

Bart was almost finished with his pancakes when a familiar face walked by the storefront, saw him sitting there, and stepped into the restaurant.

He walked right over to Bart's table and asked, "May I join you?" James Ku still had a warm smile on his face while he waited for Bart's approval to sit down.

"Of course. Please sit. I'm just about finished anyway."

"When you said you had a thing, I thought it must be business, but I can see now a hunger for food from home, yes?"

Bart acknowledged and felt embarrassed at having been found out. "I wish they had genuine Canadian syrup, but this will do in a pinch," he said while holding up a small bottle of golden syrup and trying to reinforce his Canadian persona. "What brings you this way, Mr. Ku?"

Ku explained that he recently began working for a very large travel group in New York City, and he had been sent to Beijing to scout places of interest, hotels, restaurants, and non-traditional tour sites.

He had arrived two days before Bart and had been staying in the hostel while the other beds had different people, most of them Chinese, each night. Ku was surprisingly happy to hear English being spoken, even if it was an expletive.

Bart relaxed at knowing James Ku had already been there two days when he checked in, so there was no way he was watching or following Bart.

Bart said, "I'm curious though. You surely wouldn't bring a group of American travelers all the way to Beijing to stay in triple-decker bunk beds, would you?"

Ku laughed and replied, "Maybe. I thought about the traditional trips travel customers make, and much of their expense is for hotel accommodations. I intend to meet with and tour some of Beijing's four- and five-star hotels while I am here, but I want to propose a trip that includes less elegance and more history, with more time immersed in the culture. I think it provides a richer experience than two thousand thread count sheets."

Bart thought his idea would probably not go over well because Americans like their creature comforts. But he said, "Genius idea. I love the idea of cultural immersion. How do you get around Chinese Security? Don't they tend to keep a close eye on Americans?"

"I don't see that as a problem. I wouldn't lead tours around any Government facilities or military installations. Just the sites open to tourists. I've found over fifty locations in just two days with the help of a wonderful guide that was assigned to me when I landed. I fly back in seven days, and I already have ideas for several packages I believe I can sell."

Bart congratulated James on having had a successful visit and then excused himself from the table. As he stood, James stood as well, shook his hand, and said, "If you ever find yourself in New York or need help with travel arrangements, please let me know," and handed Bart a colorful business card.

"I will definitely call you if that happens. Thank you very much. Good to have met you, James." Bart turned to leave and had another thought and asked, "Your guide, James. Is your guide with the government?"

"I hope not. He said he was with the Travel Bureau, so I thought he was an agent like me."

Bart doubted it, repeated his thanks, and walked out of the restaurant. He was amazed at how heavy the traffic on Guozijian Street was, particularly bike traffic, and even the sidewalks were full of pedestrian traffic wearing masks because of the smog. He felt like he could move about freely without being seen by whoever had entered his room at the Lijingwan International Hotel.

Being a loose end for someone as powerful and connected as Senator Chapman had Bart frightened and incredibly disappointed. He idolized the Senator and considered him a mentor and someone who, until the previous evening, he had dreamed of emulating.

All of that had been replaced by fear and a growing sense of loathing. He now found himself not only a hunted loose end but a stranger, adrift in a foreign land with no possible means of getting out. But Ira Kroonenberg didn't raise him to give up so easily, and he vowed to himself to find a way out.

Bart walked the busy streets of Beijing for several hours, trying to formulate a plan for getting back to the United States. He had his passport and credit cards, but both were too easily tracked. He thought about walking into the US Embassy on An Jia Lou Road after seeing a diplomatic vehicle drive by.

He followed it as far as the corner and watched it pull up to a gate and be admitted by guards wearing uniforms that were not American military. He watched for a while and then strolled down An Jia Lou Road and saw that it was the Israeli Embassy. He walked a little further and found the French Embassy and, finally, the US Embassy on the same street. He made a mental note of the location in case he could not find a discreet, back-channel way of getting out.

His work for the Senator required a lot of problem-solving, and he had established a great network of resources. Unfortunately, they all knew him as Bart from Senator Chapman's office, and it was the name Chapman that opened doors and gave Bart the limited influence he wielded in Washington, but he required more anonymity in this situation.

He stepped into a small café and ordered a noodle dish, and when he pulled the remaining yuan from his pocket, the business card of James Ku, Travel Coordinator for Galaxy Travel Partners, came out. Bart couldn't believe he hadn't thought of it earlier, but he was walking around in a constant state of fear.

He made his way back to the hostel and ran up the stairs to his room and found it empty. No luggage or bathroom items were left in the room, so James Ku had checked out. He walked down to the small lobby and asked the desk attendant if Mr. Ku had checked out and found that he had.

Disappointed, Bart turned to leave when the clerk said, "Mr. Ku left the name of the next hotel he's staying at," and Bart turned back with a feeling of hope.

"Could I have that?" he asked, and the clerk opened a drawer, retrieved a paper folio, and said, "Here it says, Lijingwan International Hotel."

Bart couldn't believe it. There must be over three hundred hotels in Beijing, and he wondered why that hotel? He thanked the clerk and walked out onto the bustling street, then turned left, walking in the direction of the hotel he had fled the night before.

It was after six in the early evening when Bart began crossing the park adjacent to the Lijingwan International Hotel. He stayed close to the trees that lined a jogging trail until he came to a pavilion with public restrooms and a concession stand that was closed.

He used the restroom sink to drink some water and wash his face and neck. Just outside the restroom was a payphone, and Bart had a little change from his lunch stop. There was no telephone book, and Bart couldn't read one even if there had been one, so he decided to risk a walk into the hotel.

He walked to the far side of the park and stood just one hundred feet from the front portico, waiting until the sun had gone down completely. After an hour of watching the front of the hotel, he saw an opportunity to enter.

A tourist bus had pulled into the entry circle and began unloading a group of senior citizens. They were slow and careful coming off the bus and tended to wait as the group was completed before moving as one.

Bart stepped around the front of the bus and said, "Welcome to the Lijingwan International Hotel," getting everyone's attention.

They gathered around him and walked into the lobby with Bart in the middle of the group, as the elderly new guests stepped up to four staffed positions to be checked in.

Bart stepped away and picked up a hotel brochure from a rack at the end of the counter, pretending to read it as he surveyed the lobby for threats or a familiar face. The brochure included the hotel's phone number in English.

He started to walk back out of the hotel to retrace his steps back to the payphone in the park when someone touched his shoulder. Bart's instincts and martial arts training caused him to turn with fists clenched, expecting trouble. But he spun and found the beautiful face of Lǐ Yún, the young woman from the boutique.

Her eyes widened from his reaction, and she said, "Hello, Mista Crooning Bug." Bart felt awful for the fear his reaction must have caused. He looked nervously around the lobby, crowded with people on canes and walkers, sitting in wheelchairs and milling slowly around. He could hear laughter coming from the lounge and saw the glass elevators rising with guests and returning to the lobby level.

"Ms. Yún, I mean Ms. Lĭ, it's so nice to see you again." Bart continued to look around the lobby for anyone paying attention to his presence, but nobody seemed to be looking his way. Ms. Lĭ looked around also and asked, "Who are you looking for?"

"Huh? Oh, nobody. Well, I mean, I was going to meet a friend here, but he hasn't come down yet."

"Sinta Chop Man?" she asked. Bart wanted to know where the Senator was, but he didn't want to involve this innocent young woman.

"No, Yún. Not the Senator. Another friend from America."

"Yes. Good. Sinta Chop Man left already," she said. This was news that Bart found very unsettling. It was immediately obvious that the Senator was behind whoever he had seen in his hotel room the night before. And it was also obvious the Senator had not expected Bart to return to the states with him.

It was the Senator who considered Bart to be a loose end, and Bart was on his own to survive, return to the states, and make the Senator pay for what he tried to do. He was determined to turn this loose end into the rope that hangs a powerful man.

"My friend is Mr. Ku. Do you think you... No, never mind, I will meet up with my friend later. It was nice to see you again, Ms. Lǐ," he said and started to walk away when she touched his arm again and said, "Can I walk with you?"

Bart could think of worse things than having a beautiful escort out of the hotel, so he said, "That would be great," and they walked out.

They turned toward the parking deck, and Bart walked with her as far as the elevator and said goodnight. As they walked, Bart had looked furtively over his shoulder several times, and his nervousness had not gone unnoticed.

"What frightens you, Mista Crooning Bug?"

"Hmm? Nothing. I, uh, I just didn't want to miss Mr. Ku if he..." She reached over and took his hand, and he stopped talking. "You're scared of something. I see it. How can I help you, Mista..."

"Please, Yún, call me Bart." He interrupted.

"How can I help you, Bar?" she asked, and it sounded like Bart. Bart was conflicted because he desperately needed help but had no intention of endangering her. Her language skills and the possibility of her knowing the city could be invaluable as he figured out what his next steps would be.

Bart looked around again, and, seeing nobody looking back, he asked, "Is there someplace we can go talk? Someplace away from here?"

Her smile made him feel at ease for the first time in twenty-four hours. They took the elevator up to the seventh level of the parking garage and, after a double chirp, climbed into a red compact Ande'ar.

They left the parking garage and drove for twenty minutes with very little conversation. Bart kept looking behind them, searching for anyone that might be following them. Yún Lǐ zipped in and out of lanes and avoided bicyclists who rode three abreast in a lane.

They pulled into a large parking lot the size of an American mall lot and found a spot almost a quarter mile from the nearest of three buildings that made up an apartment complex with more than one thousand units, and each building was over twenty-five stories tall.

The courtyard that sat between the three buildings was teeming with young people, and Bart reasoned that he was probably walking into housing for college students.

They entered the building farthest from the lot using a scan card and rode an elevator to the twenty-second floor, then walked down a seemingly endless and narrow hallway to Yún Lǐ's flat. It was the size of a large walk-in closet back in Washington DC.

There was a small kitchenette with a tiny, under-counter refrigerator, a microwave, and hot plate sitting on the short counter next to a sink, and a small counter extension with a single stool in front of it that separated the kitchen and sitting-sleeping area. A futon bed, made up to be a sofa, set against the window on the far wall, and a television, much too large for the space, set on the end of a desk with a single office-style chair pushed under it.

A door to his left was open, showing a darkened bathroom with a shower that reminded Bart of accommodation on a cruise ship. Yún Lǐ set her purse on the other end of the desk and dropped her keys in a dish shaped like a panda bear on his back with a basket on his chest.

She offered him a seat at the desk, and Bart said, "Nice place, Yún," and he meant it. It was not big or lavish, but it was clean, and he could tell she took pride in it. Her bed, the sofa she now sat on, had been made with no expectation of having a strange American over after work.

Yún just smiled and seemed very relaxed with Bart being there. Bart saw three bamboo tapestries hanging side by side on the wall and said, "Those are very pretty, Yún."

She looked and smiled and said, "Thank you. I made them in class. Calendars are important to honor the past and know the future. You call it the zodiac. Is this the right word?"

"Zodiac? Oh sure, yes, that's right. So, these are about the stars?" he asked because there were animals rather than constellations with which he was familiar. No Pisces or Gemini or Crab for Cancer.

"Chinese zodiac," she explained and pointed to a beautifully painted rodent on the center tapestry.

"Does 'Shŭ' mean rodent?" Bart asked.

"'Shŭ' means Rat. This is the Year of the Rat."

This made perfect sense to Bart with the sting of betrayal from Senator Chapman so fresh. His three years of dedicated service had meant nothing.

Seemingly reading his thoughts, Yún said, "Please say why you look behind when we drive and when we walk. Why you thought to strike who touched you in the hotel, if you were expecting a friend to meet you."

Bart realized how intelligent and observant Yún Li was, and he wanted very much to tell her the whole story, as he knew it then. Even more, he needed a friend, an ally who could help him.

"I'm in trouble," he said. "Not trouble with the police or the government. At least, not your government," he added.

"Trouble with Sinta Chop Man?" she asked.

"Why would you think that?"

"Because a man came in the shop last night. He said he was with Sinta Chop Man. He said he needed papers for clothing I took to your room. He said he worked for Sinta Chop Man and since Sinta paid for the clothes I gave to him. He left the store and went up the elevator to your floor. Then I didn't see him or you until tonight. Sinta left the hotel and you didn't leave with him. Strange, I think." Bart was impressed with her casual grasp of the subterfuge taking place.

"Yún, I am not sure about everything that has happened, or almost happened, but I think you are right about the Senator leaving me behind. It makes no sense, and believe me, I have tried to think of this from every angle."

"What does this mean, angle?" Yún asked.

"Every possibility. Did he get called back to Washington unexpectedly? Did something happen in his meetings that he saw as a threat and cut his visit short? Did he send that guy to my hotel room to let me know that plans have changed? Everything. And nothing makes sense."

Bart was silent for a minute, and Yún went to the kitchenette and put water in a ceramic pot, then set it on the hot plate. She pulled two cups from an open cupboard and set them on the end of the counter.

Bart asked, "The man who took the receipts and went to my room, was he Chinese? A local guy?"

"He was Chinese. He drove for big-shot customers. He had been in the hotel many times before." She thought for a moment and said, "TCL Limo Service. The sign on the car said TCL."

Bart remembered seeing TCL on the car that picked him up. Could this be the same man who drove him from the airport? The same man who had called him a loose end. If it was, as unsettling as it was to have someone looking for him, it was a relief to have seen the face of the man it could be.

Yún brought a cup of strong herbal tea over and set it on the small table between them, then sat back on the futon with her legs folded under her. "Are you going back to America now, Bar?" Everything Yún said made Bart smile. Her sweet, gentle voice made him happy, and her smile relaxed him.

"For a lot of reasons, I just can't go back right now, Yún. My passport, my credit cards, my cellphone – all of it can be tracked. I have to somehow stay off the grid."

"Grid?" Yún asked.

"Stay undetected. Out of sight until I am out of mind for anyone looking for me," he explained. "The problem is that I have no idea how to do it."

Yún took a sip of the steaming tea and said, "Yún has an idea." Bart listened intently to Yún's idea, only interjecting questions occasionally. If it could only work, he might survive and eventually get back to the States.

All it would take was his willingness to trust someone who was a stranger only a day before. But Yún seemed like a lifeline in this foreign land, and he couldn't help but want to grasp onto it with all his might.

Her plan involved him accompanying her to Yún's school the next day and meeting the Rector, another stranger he would have to trust and win over.

That was the most important step in Yún's plan, and if it worked, Bart would be going back to school. He was too much of a pragmatist and, in some ways, a pessimist to believe it could happen, but if it did, he thought, maybe surviving the Year of the Rat would be possible.

CHAPTER 10

Bart was awakened before six the next morning by a freshly scrubbed and completely dressed Yún, who gently touched his shoulder and told him he had thirty minutes to be ready to go. He rose stiffly from the mat and blankets Yún had spread on the floor for him.

Bart washed his face and freshened up as much as he could, put on his one shirt, and came out to find a cup of hot tea waiting on the kitchenette counter. He sipped it and blew on the surface to cool it and sipped again.

Yún finished her tea and opened a deep drawer next to the under-counter refrigerator and pulled a book bag out, slipped it over one shoulder, and looped the strap of her tiny purse over the same shoulder and said, "We go now, Bar?"

Bart took a last sip of tea, set his cup in the sink, and said, "Ready as I'll ever be."

The drive to China Women's University in the Chaoyang District was three miles and took almost thirty minutes in the heavy morning traffic. The sun had risen, and the yellow haze of smog was evident.

Yún and nearly everyone Bart saw along the route wore surgical masks over their faces. It occurred to Bart that wearing such a mask would help conceal his face from anyone who might be looking for him.

Yún parked in a garage near the University, and they took an elevator down to the street level with five other students who parked on the same level. Bart was smiling at the excited chatter, though he understood none of it.

They walked together to the Administration Building on Yuhui Rd, and Yún scanned a student identification card which assigned her a number, and they sat on a small sofa to wait until called. Yún had said her first class would start at nine thirty so there was no rush, having arrived before eight.

Forty minutes later, Yún's number was called, and she led Bart to the Rectorate office where a man stood in front of his desk and welcomed them in Mandarin, and then in English.

"Huänyíng, qíng lái. Welcome, please come in," Bart was surprised, not only to hear words spoken in English but with an English accent.

Yún replied, "Xèixèi lǎoshi lài kàn wǒmen. Zhè shì wǒ de péngyǒu, Bar."

Bart extended his hand and found a strong grip and a vigorous handshake, and said, "I appreciate your time, sir. Do I detect a bit of British influence there?"

The Rector was a man in his mid-forties with the first signs of salt in his pepper-colored hair, cut very short and combed meticulously. His forehead and eyes had not begun to wrinkle, and his smile was warm and friendly. He wore a double-breasted suit that was fully buttoned, yet he seemed to be very open and relaxed. His red silk tie was accented with small golden Olympic rings at various angles, and his crisp white shirt was buttoned at the collar.

"Yes, yes. Good to meet you. I am Rector Quàn Shū. Your name is Bar?" The Rector asked.

"Bart. Bart Kroonenberg," Bart corrected and smiled because he loved the way Yún spoke his name. It sounded like music to him, which made him feel at ease.

"I was educated in America at the University of Washington and then attended Cambridge. For the sake of our conversation today, let us all speak English, how would that be?" he stated. He motioned to two stuffed chairs in front of his desk and then walked around to his chair and sat down.

Yún was obviously nervous and took a deep breath before starting the conversation with the Rector.

"Lǎoshī," she began, which means teacher, and the Rector said, "Please, call me Quàn Shū. Relax and tell me how I may be of service."

Yún cleared her throat and leaned forward, and Bart could see how invested she was in his safety and appreciated how difficult this was for her. In China, women were not as free to speak their minds or to ask for special treatment. It was a totally different world than existed in the United States.

"My friend, Bar, finds himself abandoned and in need of a place to hèshēn."

"To fit in?" the Rector asked.

"Yes. Be among others. Learn and gōngzuò. Job," she said.

Yún was so nervous she went in and out of Mandarin much more than she had in previous conversations with Bart, and he felt a need to help explain his situation to take the pressure off Yún's shoulders.

"If I may, sir, I would like to explain what's going on and what I hoped you might be able to do to help me," Bart gently interrupted. He placed a hand on Yún's arm, and she blushed and looked at the floor.

"Please do. This is starting to feel like a very serious matter," Quàn Shū said. "Let's start at the beginning, shall we?"

Bart explained what had happened since the moment he landed in Beijing, sparing nothing in the way of details. When he finished he said, "I have no idea why the Senator would leave me out of meetings or leave me behind, but it seems like he didn't expect me to return with him to the United States.

He paid for my room and even some clothing from the shop at the hotel, which is how I met Yún Lǐ. When Yún told me the driver had named me Sōngsǎn de yīduān, which I thought was my name in Mandarin."

A confused look came over Quàn Shū, and he said, "This is like a thread to be pulled or sheared off."

"Yes, Yún explained it means loose end."

"Yes, yes. Even more precise. A loose end," Quàn Shū's smile faded just as Bart's had when he realized the implications of such a name. "Whose loose end, Bart, the American Senator's?"

"That's the only thing that makes sense. When I deplaned, the Senator was nowhere in sight, and the driver was standing there at the gate with my name and instructions to drive me to the hotel. The Senator had already left the airport in a different car, and the driver already knew that I was a loose end. And Yun believes the driver is the same man that came back to the hotel and went through my room."

Yún was nodding in agreement and added, "TCL man took sales paper from me."

"Yes. That's right. My name was not on any record in the hotel. My room was reserved as the Senator Chapman party, and the sales receipt was also in his name. I believe the driver returned to make sure there was no remaining trace of me at all."

It was all on the table, and the Rector sat back and exhaled a deep breath he seemed to have been holding in.

"This is a remarkable story, Mr. Kroonenberg. I would agree there seems to be some nefarious activity going on, and the Senator having abandoned you is deeply concerning, but is it a stretch to believe he wishes you harm," he asked.

"It kills me to say so, but, as hard to believe as it is, yes, I do think that's the reason for all of this."

"An unfortunate choice of words," replied the Rector.

Bart realized what he said and shrugged his shoulders and said, "I guess so, but accurate. I have worked for the Senator for three years and have never given him any reason to mistrust me. It just makes no sense."

"May I ask, do you not have your passport and the means to pay for airfare? Is this the need for which you have come to me for help?" asked Quàn Shū.

"I do have my passport, and my personal credit cards would cover the travel, but I'm concerned that both could be tracked, and by the time I landed in the States, if I'm right about the Senator's intentions, well, let's just say the possible welcome committee would not be very welcoming."

"I see. So, if your request is not financial in nature, I fail to see how I can be of any service to you. What help did you have in mind?"

Bart looked at Yún, and she took a deep breath. She leaned in and said, "Bar needs job. He has a degree and can teach English, or he can teach Politics."

Yún faltered for a moment, knowing she was asking the Rectorate to hire a foreigner to teach in a university without prior approval of the Chinese Communist Party (CCP). It was dangerous to ask and even more dangerous to put into action. Quàn Shū began shaking his head no as Yún was finishing.

Before Quàn Shū could say an emphatic no and throw them out or have them arrested, Bart said, "Not a paying job."

Both Yún and Quàn Shū looked surprised by this, and the head shaking stopped, so Bart pressed on.

"I would like to serve as a volunteer in any class you need help in, and I don't expect compensation. I understand the difficulties of hiring an American, especially one with connections to the American Government, so what I am asking of you, Quàn Shū, is to put me to work. I'll do anything, in any capacity to earn my keep while I am a guest in your beautiful country," and Bart finally took a breath.

"Perhaps you should seek a position in sales, Mr. Kroonenberg." Quàn Shū's smile had returned. "What you are asking, even as an unpaid apprenticeship, comes with significant difficulties, red tape, and certainly oversight approval by my government."

Bart was starting to feel defeated. Then Quàn Shū continued, "However, I do have a friendly contact in the Provincial Congress with whom I have worked closely, and we have worked together on an important project recently. I can reach out to her and see what might be possible."

Bart said, "I'm not familiar with the structure of your government."

"The Provincial Government is like your local government, the mayor and City Council. This may be an oversimplification, because true power is quite centralized as you might imagine, but certain members of our Provincial government are in favor right now because we are trying to host the 2002 Winter Olympics," Quàn Shū said.

He stroked the front of his tie for emphasis. "I was on the Committee, and as a result, if we do win the bid, the University will have a new ice stadium and parking facility built. Some of our student housing will be emptied and renovated to provide housing for the Olympians, so it is an exciting time for the University and for Beijing. Our committee is made up of a number of people from many levels of government. I will make discreet inquiries on your behalf."

Yún looked at her watch and said, "I must go. Art History in ten minutes. Long walk to class."

Quàn Shū stood and shook Bart's hand and said, "Leave a number where I can reach you, and I will ring you back later this week."

Yún sheepishly wrote her telephone number on Quàn Shū's tablet and said, "Bar stays with me for now. He sleeps on the floor," she quickly clarified.

"How very kind of you to accommodate Mr. Kroonenberg, Ms. Lǐ."

Bart thanked Quàn Shū, and he walked with Yún Lǐ across campus to the Arts building. Along the way, Bart asked Yún Lǐ if she trusted the Rector to help him or if he should be expecting the police to show up and arrest him.

Yún Lǐ said, without hesitation, "Quàn Shū is a good man. We trust him. He's the brother of my sensei and always tells the truth. We trust him. Do you trust me, Bar?"

Bart did. Yún directed him to a small restaurant on the campus where he could get something to eat and wait for her to finish her class. Two hours later, Bart saw her walking across the street to join him. She was walking quickly and came in the door, smiled widely when she saw Bart, and rushed over to his table and sat down.

"He called, Bar!"

"He who?" Bart was confused.

"Quàn Shū called. He wants to speak with you now," she said.

Bart could tell Yún was excited and thought such a quick turnaround was a good thing, but Bart's familiarity with how slowly the hands of government move made him skeptical and a little fearful.

He said, "I will go see him alone, Yún." He didn't want to further implicate her in whatever legal trouble he might be in. The Chinese government was well-known for their work camps, and the last thing Bart wanted to see was Yún being punished for being kind to a stranger.

"No, Bar. I'll go too. Why don't you want me to go?" she asked.

"If there is any trouble, I want you to be in the clear," he said and received a confused look. "Not clear, like transparent. I want you to be innocent of any involvement. Not in trouble."

Now she understood. "I'll go with Bar. Final say."

And that was that. Yún and Bart walked back into the Rectorate offices, scanned Yún's identification, and walked over to sit down. A few minutes later, Quàn Shū walked briskly in from the hallway, and as he passed, he motioned for Bart to follow him.

Bart looked around to see if the police were in pursuit to have caused the hurried entry but saw nobody. He and Yún walked into Quàn Shū's office, and he motioned for them to sit down as he removed his suit coat and hung it on a wooden hanger.

"I apologize if you have waited long. We had an unscheduled meeting down in the security office," this made Bart feel uneasy, until Quàn Shū continued, "we have a bicycle thief on campus, and the culprit has been caught."

Quàn Shū sat at his desk, took a deep breath, and drank from a bottle of water he had carried in.

"I spoke with my contact at Provincial Headquarters and explained as much as I believed appropriate, and, unfortunately, she cannot permit a foreigner to perform any duties for which a citizen would normally be paid. She argued convincingly that any position, work, and action benefiting the University would be seen as defrauding a member of the Party."

Bart was completely deflated and expecting the Provincial police to storm in at any moment to arrest Yún and himself.

"However, the possibility of the coming Olympics presents us, or more to the point, you with an opportunity. Although the games are six years away, should we win the bid, there is much to do to prepare our city and surrounding mountains for the arrival of more than two thousand Olympic athletes and as many support staff, not to mention world leaders and the television audience of several billion. The Olympic Committee is to let their decision be known in less than thirty days."

Bart was feeling more positive by the minute. "Where do I fit in to any of this? I'm willing to do whatever is needed."

"The Beijing Committee for Olympic Games has a need for someone to liaise with The Olympic Committees of other nations. We have such a person, my good friend Hŭa Mīng is that person. She needs someone who can speak English and can learn Mandarin to meet with world leaders. It will be heavily photographed and documented by the press."

Bart almost choked. "How can I remain hidden with the press taking photographs? Any one of those photos could end up in a newspaper or magazine or on the Internet, and anyone who's looking for me will know exactly where I am!"

"Perhaps I was wrong, but I reasoned that if someone truly is planning something awful for you, one path is to hide from them and never be free of fear. Another path is to be in public and protected. In this country, remaining in hiding is not possible for long, but having protection when you are serving the good of the Party makes it possible to discourage such threats."

Bart was skeptical, and his fear had not diminished much, but he had to trust that Hŭa Mīng would be as helpful as Quàn Shū and Yún Lĭ had been. His life was literally in their hands and now the hands of a woman he had yet to meet, but soon would.

Yún and Quàn spoke to each other in what sounded like excited Mandarin for about a minute. At the end of the conversation, Quàn wrote an address and a time on a Post-it note and handed it to Bart, who took it, looked it over, and was resigned to having his fate decided in less than twenty-four hours at the Beijing Temple of Confucius.

CHAPTER 11

Bart and Yún Lǐ left the Rectorate offices, and Bart was feeling guardedly optimistic, looking forward with hope and trepidation to his meeting the next morning with Hǔa Mīng. He could see that Yún seemed troubled and asked her about the discussion she had with Quàn Shū before they left. He told her it seemed like a disagreement.

Yún explained, "Quàn Shū said I shouldn't go with you to the meeting. He said if there's trouble, it's best I'm not there," and Bart stopped walking and turned Yún to face him. She had tears in her eyes, and he knew how badly she wanted to help and protect him.

"Quàn Shū is right, Yún. You have already done so much for me, and if there is any possibility of tomorrow's meeting going sideways."

Bart could see confusion come over her face, "If anything bad might happen, I can't let you get caught up in my mess. My trouble has to be my trouble, not your trouble." He felt like he had explained it as best he could.

Yún just looked at him and said, "I go with. Final say," and walked away in the direction of the parking garage.

Bart awoke early the next morning before dawn's light shone into the tiny room. He went quietly into the bathroom to freshen up and was thankful for the stop they had made at a small market where he picked up toiletries.

He emerged fifteen minutes later, intending to leave Yún's apartment and find his way to the Temple of Confucius without her.

He stepped into the main room and waited a moment to let his eyes adjust to the darkness after being in the brightly lit bathroom.

When he could see again, he was startled to see Yún standing in the kitchen with a cup of tea in her hands and a fierce look in her eyes. Another steaming cup of tea sat on the countertop for Bart.

"Where are you going so early, Bar?" she asked rhetorically.

Bart actually stuttered and reiterated what he had told her the previous afternoon and the night before as they both settled into their places to sleep. She never wavered in her insistence that she would go with him.

Bart realized that she was dressed and ready to go, and arguing with her was useless. He took a sip of the tea and complimented her on its flavor, and she rolled her eyes as if to say, "knock it off and be straight with me."

"You can take me to the meeting, Yún, but only if you agree to wait in the car. If the meeting goes well, I will signal you to join me. Only when I know for certain there is no danger to you. Do you understand?" Yún shook her head to say yes, she understood.

"How will you speak to Hŭa Mīng, Bar? She needs an English speaker. She doesn't speak English. You don't speak Chinese. How will you know if the meeting is going well if you can't understand Hŭa Mīng, and she can't understand you?"

Bart felt like Yún had held back her best argument for when she needed it most, and it made him smile like so many things about her did.

"You win, Yún. I do need you there. It isn't enough to have a translator. I have to have a translator I trust that will tell me exactly what is being said and, as much as possible, will translate what I'm saying accurately."

Yún looked at Bart and smiled a very big smile and asked, "What do I win, Bar?"

Bart and Yún arrived at the Beijing Temple of Confucius thirty minutes ahead of the nine a.m. meeting with Hŭa Mīng and found the entrance to the main parking lot closed to the public.

Yún drove down Guozijian Street and turned right on Jianchang Hu Tong and found the side entry to the parking closed as well. She turned left and found a fruit market with a parking lot and pulled in.

Bart was growing more concerned than before, finding so many roadblocks to the meeting place, but Yún tried to convince him that the blockades meant nothing more than the Temple was not open yet. They went into the fruit market so Yún could tell the proprietor that she would be leaving her car in the otherwise empty lot for a short time.

He seemed agreeable, and Yún said, "Xièxiè nǐ," and Bart said, "Thank you, sir."

They walked up Yongkang Hu Tong street and between two office buildings and came out on the road bordering the parking lot of the Temple of Confucius. The temple was fronted by cobblestones that Bart thought were probably hundreds and maybe thousands of years old.

Beautiful oak trees lined the entry plaza, and gas lanterns stood in front of each one to light the walkway after the sun went down. A canal encircled the holy temple, and ornate concrete barriers lined the canal and the main entrance.

Benches sat along a chained fence, and a woman dressed in a cream-colored business suit with a knee-length skirt and matching jacket was sitting on one. She wore a navy-blue silk scarf knotted in front, and very practical black leather flats. Her black hair was cut short and barely covered her ears. A small purse with a long, thin strap rested in her lap.

She looked all business yet friendly at the same time. Bart looked beyond her to the surrounding area for any possible threats and saw only a few workmen on scaffolds cleaning the temple's exterior. Feeling it was safe, Bart said, "Okay, Yún, let's go see if this is Hŭa Mīng and get this over."

As they approached, the woman saw them walking her way and stood from the bench and smiled warmly and said, "Zăoshang hăo," and Yún said it back to her, and then for Bart's benefit, she said, "Good morning."

Bart said, "Good morning, Ms. Ming, it is an honor to meet you. My name is Bart Kroonenberg."

Hŭa Mīng smiled and looked to Yún, who translated for her. Ming said, "Xièxiè. Ràng wŏmen biān zŏubiān liáo Bar," and Yún immediately told Bart they would walk with her.

They walked at a very leisurely pace, and Hŭa Mīng listened as Yún explained Bart's predicament. She concluded with her own declaration of full support for the

Party and how humbled and honored she was to be able to speak with such an esteemed woman of power within the CCP.

Hŭa Mīng was used to acolytes who showed respect but was particularly touched by what Yún had said, seeing how much she cared for this black American man whom she had only known for three days. She reasoned that Yún must be a good judge of a man's character to risk her freedom and safety to help him in this manner.

Having explained everything as they walked slowly around the plaza, Hŭa Mīng pointed to a small table with four chairs set along the chain perimeter fence, and they walked over and sat down. Bart had not spoken a word after the initial greeting, and nothing had been translated as yet, so he surmised what was being said simply by tone inflection.

When they had sat, Hŭa Mīng looked directly into Bart's eyes and said, "Bart, wŏ jiāng xiàng nín jiěshì sān Zhŏng kĕnég xing," then looked at Yún, who translated to Bart that Hŭa Mīng says there are three possible paths to take. Bart acknowledged by nodding and looking back to Hŭa Mīng.

The conversation continued with Yún translating for Bart and for the government official offering Bart some very interesting choices. The first path was the most difficult because Bart would have to present himself to the proper authorities to explain why he was in the country and no longer on US government business.

This choice carried the highest threat level because the Chinese Communist Party may determine that Bart is an American Spy and simply arrest him and sentence him to a work camp for who knows how long. If the party believed Bart and did not believe he was there to spy for the Americans, then he would be able to work with Hŭa Mīng as a liaison for the Olympic effort.

She had said her committee was very hopeful they would win the bid to bring the 2002 Winter Olympics to Beijing, and his skills as a diplomat would be invaluable to the party. This path had a second possible pitfall Bart had to be aware of. If the International Olympic Committee did not choose Beijing as the host, his services would not be needed, and his presence in the country might again be scrutinized.

Path two was for Bart to present himself to a party official and renounce his American citizenship, effectively defecting to China. Having worked in government since graduating from college, it might be believed that Bart had helpful information for the Chinese Communist Party. Jiang Zemin, the current paramount leader of China, is known to be a zealous party champion and willing to accept defectors who have value to the CCP.

As soon as Bart heard option two, he began shaking his head and said, "Respectfully, ma'am, I could never—would never renounce my American citizenship. I would rather go to a work camp." No translation was necessary, and Hŭa Mīng shook her head to indicate she understood.

Path three was the most unexpected - a direction he never expected to come up as a possibility. Hŭa Mīng had a brother whose son had entered a temple four years earlier, and when she had visited him recently, there were two Americans there who were Secular disciples. They had been welcomed by the monks, and when the monks traveled, they were able to travel freely and with their monastic names. They enjoyed complete anonymity.

The CCP does not exercise any control over the monasteries, and the monks enjoy more freedom than other citizens because of the reverence the people and the government have for them.

Bart smiled and said, "I'm not sure I see myself as a monk, but this path seems like the safest. Would you agree?"

Yún looked at Bart as though she didn't want to translate because she didn't want him to take this path. It was a path that would completely remove him from her life, and he had become very important to her. She finally resolved that any path taken must be the one best and safest for Bart and not the one most pleasing for her.

"Zhè tiáo lù zuì ānquán ma, Bart?" she asked.

Hŭa Mīng said that it was and that she would be happy to make the introduction to the abbot of the local temple. If Bart were accepted to the sect, he would follow the path her nephew had taken, which was to go to the main temple some eight hundred kilometers away, where his studies and training would take place. It was a commitment of years, not months.

Bart had grown up in a Jewish household with a mother who was much more committed to Judaism than his father, but she had influenced Bart to be faithful to the Torah.

As an adult, Bart had been more career-focused and had not been to the temple in a couple of years. But could he actually turn his back on it and become a Buddhist? He didn't think he could. Could he live dishonestly among monks who commit their lives to the sect? He didn't think that was possible either.

Bart decided that honesty and integrity were just too important to the man he was and said, "I think the best path for me to take is to present myself and my situation to a CCP official and accept however they want to deal with me."

Bart looked at Yún and smiled at the earnest look on her face as she waited for him to decide. "I cannot be dishonest, and I do not want to hide in your country. I have too much respect for law and custom to do that."

Bart knew he would be putting his freedom at serious risk by his decision, but having said what he did, he was finally able to exhale. He would accept whatever came his way, and his actions would not further endanger Yún Lǐ.

Yún looked at Bart with what he thought was a mix of gratitude and agreement, and she smiled and turned to face Hǔa Mīng. She translated what Bart had said and concluded with, "Bar is a good man."

Hǔa Mīng smiled as she heard the translated message and began to shake her head affirmatively. When Yún had finished, Hǔa Mīng said, "Xièxiè" to her and then to Bart she said, "A wise choice."

Bart was stunned to hear her speak so clearly in his language. Yún's eyes enlarged, and she was clearly surprised.

"I am an official CCP authority you have presented to, Bart. Let us see how we may help one another."

CHAPTER 12

The following two weeks were a mental endurance test, with Bart working endless hours trying to learn Mandarin from a CD set provided by Hŭa Mīng. He came to her office in the Government sector each morning, where she met him outside at a transit stop and escorted him into her office.

The paramount leader of China, Jiang Zemin, had an office in the building next door, and security was extremely high. Every time Zemin left his office, the front door was guarded until after his motorcade left the large circular drive.

Bart sat in a small cubicle with a headset and a cassette recorder with a microphone attached. He repeated the words spoken into the headphones and then played his words back for Hŭa Mīng during a one-hour review session each afternoon. She invited Yún Lĭ to join them as often as possible, but being a full-time student and working at the boutique in the hotel kept her busy, and Bart had asked that she not expose herself to any further scrutiny by CCP officials.

Bart had asked for access to a computer with an Internet connection, wanting to let his parents know where he was and that he was safe, but permission had been denied. It frustrated him, but he respected Hŭa Mīng's authority and appreciated her looking out for him.

He had been in Beijing for almost three weeks, and he rarely went three days without calling his mother, and about half of the calls ended up being on speaker with both parents involved in the discussion. He missed them and knew they would be worried about him, and he was concerned they might contact Senator Chapman to find out where he was. He didn't want them to have any interaction with the Senator.

Bart would take the cassettes home to Yún's apartment. She would listen and point out many of the same things Hŭa Mīng did to make his language skills more conversational and dialectically accurate for the region. They would speak lines back and forth as Bart tried, with a very practiced ear, to emulate her accent and inflection to speak Mandarin with the authenticity of dialect.

At the end of Bart's third week of language immersion, Hŭa Mīng came by his cubicle late afternoon and asked him to visit her office. Bart settled into an offered chair, and Hŭa Mīng asked him to wait momentarily.

There was a light tap on the door, and Hŭa Mīng opened it and ushered Yún into the room where she sat next to Bart. He was happy to see her but confused about why she was there. Hŭa sat down behind her big mahogany desk and, for a moment, moved a stapler aside and gathered some scattered papers into a neat pile, then took a drink from a teacup. Bart had the feeling she was stalling or dreading the conversation, and he soon found he was right.

"Bart, I asked Yún to be here to give news to both of you now," she said, and then set her cup down with a shaking hand.

"What is it, Ms. Mīng? Has something happened?" Bart asked, and the tension in the room was palpable. Bart was getting very concerned for his and Yún's safety.

Hŭa began speaking quickly in Mandarin, looking back and forth between Bart and Yún, and Bart actually understood some of the words even at the rapid rate with which they were spoken. He picked up on premier, responsible, punishment, and no time. The rest was an audio blur he couldn't hope to understand yet. He looked at Yún whose face revealed the fear she felt, and when Hŭa finished speaking, Yún looked at Bart with tears beginning to roll from both eyes.

"International Olympic Committee did not choose Beijing to host the games. They chose an American city, Salt Lake," Bart understood what she meant and said, "Jìxù qĭng. Continue, please."

"Premier Jiang Zemin holds the Beijing Olympic Committee member personally responsible for the insult and failure. Hŭa Mīng must report to the premier's office tomorrow. She thinks maybe she won't come back. She says you and I must go far away now."

Bart never anticipated a setback so monumental when this path was first taken. He thought being aligned with someone in a powerful and influential position worked in his favor. He had not figured on the ego of a leader being bruised by the IOC's decision.

Hǔa and Quàn Shū were both so confident that Beijing would win the bid to host the Olympics, it never occurred to Bart that they might be wrong, or the possible consequences of that miscalculation. Even more, Bart was deeply concerned about the safety of Yún Lǐ, Hǔa Mīng, and Quàn Shū. They had all been so kind and helpful to him, and he genuinely liked them. As much as it frightened him to admit it, he was probably in love with Yún.

"How do we handle this? What can we do? Bìxū zuò shénme?" Bart asked.

"Néng zuò de dōu zuò wánliǎo. Nothing more can be done, Bart," Hǔa Mīng replied dejectedly. She was a strong woman, and Bart had liked her from their first meeting and respected her more and more as they trained together.

He could see that she had resigned herself to whatever outcome the CCP Premier would arrive at for punishment over this loss of face on the world stage. "The time now is for you and Yún Lǐ to go. You must not be here tomorrow when decisions are made. You understand, yes?"

Bart understood perfectly. He had worked for three years for a man who, it turned out, was capable of abandoning his aide in a communist country, and who knows what else. He knew that people with power exercised that power in ways most people could not imagine.

"Shì de wǒ míngbái. I understand," Bart replied. "But there must be something we can do to help you. You have been so kind and so helpful, Huā Mīng."

"Bart. That is my crime," she said. "I helped an American. An American city will host the Olympics, not Beijing. It looks bad. You must go far away with this," she said and pulled an envelope out of her top drawer and laid it on the desk in front of Bart. "This will get you to Taiwan, and from there you can get back to America. You must take Yún Lǐ with you. You understand this, Bart?"

"Shì de wǒ míngbái," Bart said. He understood the grave situation they were in. He picked up the envelope and started to pull out the contents, but Huā Mīng stopped him with a wave of her hand.

"Not to open now, Not here," she said. "I have found understanding of why Yún Lǐ trusts you and wants to help you. It pleases me to have known you, and if I can help you get back to your home, it is my honor, Bart Kroonenberg." She stood and came around the desk, signaling their discussion was over and it was time to go. She embraced Bart who hugged her tightly and didn't try to hide the tears he shed. She then hugged Yún Lǐ and wished her well. She spoke gently in Mandarin as Yún stood there nodding her understanding and let the tears flow. Bart took Yún's hand, and they walked out the door, glancing back and giving a final wave of goodbye to their friend and benefactor, Huă Mīng.

In Yún's car, driving back to her apartment, Bart opened the envelope and found a stack of Chinese yuan that he calculated to be a little over five thousand U.S. dollars. There were two letters folded up on either side of the currency written entirely in Chinese characters Bart had no hope of reading. When they pulled into the parking lot of Yún's apartment complex thirty minutes later, Bart handed the two letters to Yún to read for him. She looked at one and then the other and said, "The letter gives permission to go to Taiwan. It says you and I are emissaries – representing Huă Mīng's office with diplomatic passage," Yún said. She turned to look at Bart and asked, "Do you want Yún to go with you?"

Bart smiled at the familiar melodic way Yún still said his name and the innocent look on her beautiful face, and his heart was filled to overflowing in spite of the danger they may have been in. "I want nothing more than to have you with me, Yún. Is that something you want? It may be difficult to ever come back to Beijing once we get out," he explained.

He knew it was not a decision to be made easily or taken lightly. He had been away from his home country for less than a month, and the feeling of hopelessness mixed with homesickness was never far from his mind.

"Yún is happy with Bar. Parents have been dead in a work camp for a long time. I want to go with Bar. We go now."

Bart helped Yún pack a few things, and he packed the few belongings he had accumulated during his short time in the country. She pulled her passport out of the kitchen drawer where she kept her book bag, and then pulled a favorite book of art pieces out of the bag to take with her.

Bart and Yún bought tickets to Taiwan at a kiosk in the Beijing International Airport. They walked with trepidation to the Customs station and expected to be taken aside and questioned, but getting through customs was much easier once Bart and Yún presented their letters of passage provided by Hūa Mīng. The official stamp of her Office of Commerce carried sway with the Inspectors.

They walked to the large conveyor belt for people movement that moved the thousands of people in the terminals from gate to gate. They moved swiftly to their gate and then spent a fearful two hours waiting for their China Airlines flight.

They boarded in the first group in coach seating and settled in for the direct flight, which was supposed to take just over two and a half hours. It was just past eleven pm when their flight was finally airborne, and Yún held tightly to Bart's hand until the Fasten Seatbelt sign was turned off. The flight was smooth, and the snack service was appreciated because neither Bart nor Yún had eaten since lunchtime.

The landing at Taipei, Taiwan was a little bumpy with crosswinds causing the airplane to move sideways, and Yún again was squeezing tightly to Bart's hand and had her eyes closed in apparent prayer. Bart just smiled and was thankful for the safe landing and for the woman sitting next to him.

When the doors of the aircraft were opened, and they walked by the flight attendant saying, "Xièxiè" to everyone as they passed, Bart felt the sweet embrace of freedom for the first time in a month. Bart's work with Senator Chapman, who chaired the Senate Foreign Relations Committee, made him very familiar with the treaties in place with this most important ally in the Pan-Pacific. They walked up the ramp from the Boeing 737 to the brightly lit and almost empty terminal in the Taiwan Taoyuan International Airport. Their baggage found its way to the downstairs carousel within twenty minutes, and they went out to find transportation to a hotel.

The weather was muggy and warm, and the smell of wet pavement was strong after a rain shower had come through. They stood at the curb, exhausted from the long day and all that had happened, and feeling hopeful for the future. A very new feeling for both of them.

A yellow Nissan pulled to a stop, and the driver jumped out and rounded the back of the vehicle as the trunk lid was opening, took their luggage and placed it inside as they climbed into the back of the car.

Yún spoke to the driver and asked him to take them to the nearest hotel, and he pulled away from the curb and started his meter. They rode in silence with Yún resting her head on Bart's shoulder and still holding his hand. Ten minutes later they pulled into a circular driveway in front of the Sheraton Taoyuan Hotel.

Bart made three calls from the hotel, the last one to book a flight on Singapore Airlines to New York, New York, through Honolulu, Hawaii. Then he booked a separate flight out of Honolulu to Charleston, West Virginia on American Airlines using Yún's credit card. Although he felt free and safe where he was, he didn't dare drop his guard until he and Yún were safe and sound on American soil and fully understood what Senator Chapman was up to.

The second call was to his cousin Jaime in Pittsburgh, Pennsylvania, to whom Bart had not spoken for nearly four months. The cousin confirmed what Bart believed had happened. The entire Kroonenberg family believed Bart had disappeared without a trace. Senator Chapman had been asked in the press about his missing Aide, and he had responded that, "His thoughts and prayers are with Bartholomew's family, and he hoped that whatever was keeping him away would all work out, and he would come back safely."

What a phony! Bart thought. He asked his cousin to keep his return a secret but asked him to drive to Philadelphia to meet with his parents in person and to take them away from their house to tell them he was fine and coming home soon. He gave very specific instructions Jaime was to tell his parents.

Bart went down to the lobby while Yún took a shower, and while there, he stepped into the business center and logged into a computer. It was the first time he had access to the Internet, and he did searches for his name, Senator John Chapman news, and Global Achievements.

He found an article declaring him as a missing person, several articles about the Senator and various bills and committees he was involved with. He read the heartfelt phony statement he had made regarding Bart's disappearance. He found dozens of articles about activities Global Achievements was spearheading. It seemed they were involved with every bill Senator Chapman had written or signed onto for the last ten years. They were deeply involved with tobacco, tort reform, medical insurance, big pharmaceutical and many others. Bart knew them to be purveyors of influence within the halls of congress but didn't realize the extent.

Bart was getting ready to shut down the computer, and he had a thought, so he reopened the Internet browser and did a search for Dr. Patrick Rivera of Dallas, Texas. The search results were extensive. There was a doctor of Internal Medicine in North Dallas, and the profile picture showed an elderly man with privileges at Presbyterian Hospital. There was another listing for a Dr. Patrick Rivera who didn't seem to have hospital privileges or a practice from what he could tell. The last listing was the one that caused the hair to stand up on the back of his neck. It was an obituary for a thirty-two-year-old doctor of internal medicine who tragically died of a heart attack while playing golf in Reston, Virginia. The doctor was unmarried but was survived by his father and a long list of family and extended family members, including two of the other listed Dr. Patrick Rivera's. Bart wrote the office number of the elderly doctor on a Sheraton notepad, folded it, and put it in his wallet, and closed up the computer.

    The third call was to Dallas, and Bart was able to speak with the office manager who said the doctor would call him back when he returned from doing rounds at the hospital. Bart explained that he was traveling and would call back another time. Yún finished her shower and came out in a white terry cloth robe with Sheraton embroidered over the left breast area. Her hair was wrapped in a towel, and she smelled of flowers as she walked by.

Their relationship had not progressed beyond holding hands and comforting hugs, and neither believed now was the time to go to the level their hearts desired. Now was the time for mental clarity and no new complications.

They slept in the two full-size beds in the room and awoke before dawn for their 8 am flight to Honolulu. They arrived eleven hours later and got a room at the Waikiki Hilton and had dinner and some rest for their flight out the next afternoon.

They spent time in Hawaii as a couple of people in their twenties who had recently found, what they believed to be, true love. They walked on the beach at sunset and then sat by a hotel pool talking. Along their walks and quiet time together, Bart continued to improve and expand his linguistic perfection, begun by Hŭa Mīng. At the same time, Yún was working on her English, and she, too, was improving little by little. Bart enjoyed the work and hoped Yún would never learn to correctly say his name, thoroughly enjoying the way she said it.

They returned to their hotel room just before 11 pm and settled in for a good night's sleep, but sleep wouldn't come. They talked well into the night about what life was like in Philadelphia, Pennsylvania, where Bart's parents lived, and where he would likely return. He was certain that doors would not remain open to him in Washington DC and felt like it was time to pursue other possibilities. Politics had been his passion, but the seedy side of the game left him wanting. After talking for hours, Yún got up and went into the bathroom.

The lack of conversation gave Bart a moment to close his eyes, and he had just about drifted off to sleep when Yún's sweet, gentle voice said, "I lay with Bart?" and Bart was instantly awake. She stood next to his bed in a silky nightgown with cherry blossoms imprinted on the sleeves, with outstretched arms and a beautiful smile on her face. Bart lifted his blanket and sheet and welcomed her into his bed. They embraced, and he kissed her for the first time. It was the first time since they had met that tomorrow didn't scare them beyond words. She kissed him eagerly and then said, "Please hold for comfort. We sleep, yes?" Bart's body wanted to argue and beg for more, but his heart and mind knew better and respected Yún's desire. He held her close as sleep finally came.

Bart watched the sunrise from the small balcony while sipping the first cup of coffee in over a month. He had run everything through his mind that he thought may lay ahead, trying to imagine every possible scenario. He knew Senator Chapman to be a very resourceful man and had come to realize he was also ruthless. It could be a coincidence that the man he was supposed to play golf with and was told to cancel on had died of a sudden heart attack at just thirty-two years of age. Bart dismissed that possibility because he didn't believe in coincidences. There were too many CDC and WHO scientists involved in the meetings at Global Achievements with the Senator, all of whom had access to poisons and toxins, to believe a young man who had caught the Senator's attention one day and was dead the next, died of natural causes. No matter what the Coroner's report claimed because Coroners can be bought just like anyone else.

The Asian man Bart had seen at the table when Bart had given the Senator a note had also been to the Senator's office in Richmond a couple of times. Bart had been introduced to him and believed his name was Tong or Tang or Tau but wasn't certain. He knew he was in a position of authority with a laboratory somewhere in China, but again, nothing was certain.

When people began walking out to the pool deck nineteen stories below him, Bart stepped inside the room, and Yún was sitting on the edge of the bed, stretching her arms above her head and yawning. Bart said, "Sleep okay?" and she smiled and replied, "sleep good."

They had an hour before they had to catch the hotel shuttle over to the airport twenty minutes away. Bart kissed Yún good morning and said he had to make a call. He sat at the desk and dialed a Dallas number. When Dr. Rivera came on the line, Bart explained who he was and that, with mutual friends, he was supposed to play golf with Dr. Patrick Rivera, but the game had been canceled.

The elderly doctor was still grieving and a little impatient, and asked, "I'm not sure why you're calling me or what you want from me, but I don't have time for this."

Bart apologized for having bothered him and said, "I just have some suspicions about the way it happened, and quite honestly, I'm not convinced it was a heart attack."

The old man responded, "Now you're sounding like my nephew. Why don't you call him and the two of you can share your concerns. I just buried the cremated remains of my youngest child and quite frankly, I'm not interested in conspiracy theories." He provided the office number for his nephew and hung up the phone.

Bart's next call was answered by a switchboard operator at Warner Pharmaceuticals, who put him through to the office of Dr. Patrick Rivera. Pat answered the call, and Bart quickly identified himself.

"It's about time you called me back!"

"I beg your pardon. This is Bart Kroonenberg from Virginia," Bart responded.

"Yes, I know, and I left a message for you more than three weeks ago. What took so long for a simple courtesy call?"

Bart was confused and said, "Ok. Let's back this up a bit. Let me explain why I'm calling you and where I have been for the last month. Then maybe we can get somewhere." Bart went through some of the events of the previous month, beginning with the order to cancel the golf game and to discontinue seeing his friends, to being literally Shanghaied and deserted in Beijing.

"Now let me fill in some blanks for you because you just filled in a couple for me." Pat told of his frustrating and frightening trip to Virginia to identify and claim his cousin's body. He told of the fictitious Asian attorney who changed the directive, causing his cousin's body to be cremated, and lastly, he told Bart about having worked with Detective Sergeant Gary Saunders, who for some unknown reason, had driven to Richmond, Virginia where he was murdered and set on fire. He added that the Herndon Police Department had reassigned Detective Saunders cases to a Detective Williams, who dismissed him completely, saying there was no investigation and there was no murder. Nobody had any idea why Saunders had driven to Richmond.

"Maybe something had led him to Senator Chapman," Bart suggested. "He has an office there."

"I don't know. We'll never know because all of his notes were burned with him."

Bart told Pat that he was flying back to the states in a couple of hours, and he would touch base with him in a few days when he figures out his next moves.

Pat said, "You have no idea how much this means to me. I want to help, and before you say no, I'm a trained investigator. Well, sort of. I am a scientist, and I am very methodical, and two minds are better than one when solving a dilemma, wouldn't you agree?"

Bart did, and he said so, but he also said he didn't want to endanger anyone else with what he had to do. The Senator had left him in China to be imprisoned or even killed, and he had to make the Senator pay for that. Knowing that he may also have had something to do with an innocent man's death made it all the more critical that Bart stop him.

"I can leave tomorrow and meet you in Reston or Richmond, whichever you prefer. Let me help. If we're right, the Senator is behind as many as four murders. Let's stop him before there are any more."

"Okay. It will be good to have some help, but we have to be very careful. The Senator is more dangerous than anything in your lab, trust me," Bart said. "Can you fly to Philadelphia tomorrow?"

"No problem."

Bart got Patrick's cellphone number and promised to call him the next day. He asked him to get a room at the Residence

Inn in Wynnefield Heights, and he would meet up with him in the evening the next day.

Bart disconnected and gathered up his belongings, repacked his bag, and he and Yún went down to catch the shuttle. He was sickened to think that his former boss, a man he had looked up to for three years, could be instrumental in four deaths. His determination to stop him grew by the minute.

Chapter 13

Bart and Yún walked out of Yeager Airport in Charleston, West Virginia, and waited for the shuttle to take them to the Hertz Rental Car office. They rented a Chevrolet Impala and began their drive to Philadelphia. Bart's parents had been relieved beyond imagination at the news their nephew had brought.

His father had agreed to Bart's request and bought a cell phone that his cousin had called a burner and given the number to Jaime who then gave it to Bart when he called from Hawaii. Bart stopped at a department store and purchased a phone and had one hundred minutes of use added to it. Back in the car, Bart telephoned his parents who answered on the second ring.

Bart's emotions threatened to boil over at hearing his father's voice, "Dad, it's me. Please don't say my name out loud, but God, it's good to hear your voice," he said and choked back tears.

"Likewise, more than you can imagine," his father said, and Bart could hear the same emotions there. "Is there somewhere we can talk?" asked his father.

"Yes. But not yet. I have a few things to do first, and I have to remain out of sight and out of mind to be able to do them. It won't be long, I promise," Bart said. "Is mom there?"

"Not at the moment, but if possible, we could call you together later this afternoon?"

"Yes, but to be safe, please do it away from your house and not in your car. I know I'm being overly cautious, and I'll explain it all when I can."

"We welcome that. There is so much we want to know."

"I love you, Dad. For now, just know that. And Mom too, please tell her. I'll talk to you soon. Goodbye for now." Bart hung up the phone, and Yún squeezed his arm and rubbed his neck as he drove down the freeway toward Philadelphia.

Bart had converted their remaining yuan to US dollars in Honolulu, and they had a little over two thousand remaining. The drive to Philadelphia took them nine hours, stopping for fuel and food along the way. They arrived in Wynnefield Heights, a northern suburb of Philadelphia and got a room at the Residence Inn. Bart asked if Dr. Rivera had checked in yet and found that he had not.

They drove to a local mall, and Bart found what he needed at a Radio Shack.

They went to a large department store, and Yún picked out some clothing that was more western than anything she owned so she would fit in. Bart thought she was beautiful in whatever she wore, but her happiness was most important to him. He discussed what he planned to do next, and Yún understood why he needed to.

They walked the length of the mall's main corridor and then down a couple of wings that were full of smaller shops and boutiques until Bart found what he was looking for. He waited until called and took a seat, explained what he wanted to an amused stylist who proceeded to shave Bart's head completely.

He looked in the mirror and didn't recognize himself, so he doubted the Senator would either, but he wanted to go one step further. Yún had been watching from the lobby as Bart was transformed and her smile was wide and full-faced as he emerged, rubbing his smooth scalp as he walked.

"Bar like Shaolin Monk," and she kept smiling.

He paid in cash then he and Yún walked the corridors looking for a store he wasn't sure the mall would have, and they didn't. He went back to the Radio Shack and asked to use one of the display computers to do a quick Internet search and found what he was looking for just three miles away.

Ichabod's Costume shop sat at the end of a strip mall facing a side street and looked like it would soon go out of business. It smelled of cigarette smoke, and there was something sticky on the floor just off the welcome mat. The front window had a suit of armor and a court jester's costume on mannequins, and above the checkout counter, there was a Wizard of Oz Dorothy costume on a child-sized mannequin.

The shelves had plastic swords, plastic rifles, cavalry uniforms, and French maid costumes along with a purple Barney and a Big Bird costume that seemed too big to wear.

The man at the counter was unfriendly and unhelpful and barely looked up from the newspaper he was reading. Bart found what he was looking for on metal hooks on an endcap that tilted badly to one side and had more empty hooks than products. Pickings were slim, but Bart reasoned that the fake beard and mustache didn't have to match his real hair because he no longer had any. He paid for his disguise and left the disgusting shop in the rearview mirror.

Bart went back to the hotel and called the burner phone to speak with his father. After one ring, a very anxious and instantly emotional answer came from his mother on speaker so his father could hear everything.

"Mom, please don't say my name. It's me, I'm OK."

"Bartuch Ata Adonai, Eloheinu Melech Haolam, shehechiyanu, v'kiy'manu, v'higianu lazman hazeh," his mother quickly uttered. Bart recognized her words as a Jewish blessing he had heard many times growing up.

"I have worried until I am sick, my boy. God has brought you back to me," she added, and Bart could tell she was crying and on the verge of sobbing. He looked at Yún who looked completely lost at the language she was hearing.

"Mom I really need you to not say my name while you're at home or in your car until I know the extent of the threat," Bart said.

"Your father and I have been at East Fairmont Park for three hours waiting to hear from you. I think it's safe to talk. Where are you? Where have you been? Why haven't you called us before today?" The questions were coming rapid fire, and he knew they deserved answers.

"Mom. Just give me a few minutes, and I'll tell you everything. I love you both so much. Where are you at the park?"

"We are sitting at a picnic table under a shade tree near the east parking lot. Why?"

"I'm coming to you. Stay right there."

A mother's hug is like no other, and the one Bart found himself locked in was threatening his ability to breathe. And he loved it. His father wrapped his arms around both of them, and it was the safest Bart had felt in a long time. The embrace ended, and his mother wanted to meet the young woman with Bart.

"This is Yún. She saved my life," Bart said, and the door was opened for them to hear everything that had happened over the last thirty-four days.

Leaving nothing out, Bart told his parents about everything from the time he handed a message to Senator Chapman who was having dinner at Global Achievements until the moment they landed in Charleston.

After hearing the full story, both his parents were thankful for his safety, thankful for the help Yún had given him and for the Commerce Director in Beijing who had given them the means to get out of China.

Bart's mother wanted to know how serious their relationship was, which embarrassed Bart and made Yún blush.

Bart's father simply said, "I told you three years ago not to trust a Democrat."

Bart explained what his next moves were and asked if Yún could stay with them while he went to Washington DC. Yún was reluctant to separate from Bart but she trusted his wisdom and knew she could use the time to get to know his parents, and they her. They spent over an hour talking and laughing, crying, and hugging and laughing some more. Bart wanted desperately to just stay with them and forget everything else he knew he must do, but he wasn't made that way.

When they left the park, Bart kissed Yún and told her he would be back to get her soon and to stay strong. "Keep working on your English and I promise to keep working on my Mandarin.

Zàijiànle, wǒ de àirén, bye for now Yún."

"Farewell, Bar. Yún love Bar with whole heart."
Bart's mother locked arms with Yún and said, "I think you and I are going to get along just fine." Then she kissed Bart on his cheek, hugged him, and said, "You be safe. Don't take any unnecessary risks and make that SOB pay for leaving you behind."

## CHAPTER 14

When Bart returned to the hotel, the red light was flashing on the telephone in his room, indicating there was a message waiting for him. He checked and found that Dr. Rivera had checked in and provided a room number. They arranged to meet in the lobby to go to dinner.

Over Italian dishes at a local restaurant Bart was familiar with, they talked about the next steps they needed to take. Bart felt better having the help of someone other than Yún because he worried about her safety to the point it could become distracting.

Also, the trained researcher had some ideas about getting to the Senator that Bart had not considered. They agreed to try one of them and decided to meet early the next morning, return one of the rental cars, and make a drive during which they will nail down every step of the plan.

The drive to Washington DC took a little over four hours, including a brief stop for fuel and fast-food sandwiches Bart and Pat ate on the way. They talked through the part each would play in the master plan Pat had come up with. He wanted to use the notoriety of Bart's disappearance to their benefit, which Bart had not considered. He had thought it best to stay in hiding, going so far as to change his appearance. That change, however, could also be useful to them in the execution of the plan.

They arrived in Washington DC and got two rooms in Foggy Bottom at a hotel near George Washington University. Graduation commencement had just concluded, so they had no trouble finding rooms. However, the fourth of July celebration had just concluded as well, and there were a lot of people in town, so restaurants were busier than usual. There were also press vans all over the city, which was not unusual for Washington DC.

Bart got a table at the Athena Greek Restaurant around the corner from the NBC office and waited as Patrick walked over and entered the lobby. A young receptionist greeted him, and he asked to speak with Tom Roberts, the host of the long-running Sunday News show, Meet the Press.

It wasn't going to be that easy, unfortunately. The receptionist said she could take a message and see if a member of his staff could contact him. Patrick said it was a matter of life and death and if Tom wasn't available he would just go over to the Fox News office.

Fox News had just recently launched a Sunday news program with Chris Wallace, and Patrick was sure he would be interested in the scoop Patrick was offering. He planted that seed and then turned to leave the lobby when the receptionist stopped him and asked him to wait a moment.

This was an integral part of Patrick's plan because he had seen promotional trailers for the Sunday show and knew that Senator John Chapman was going to be interviewed. Bart took a seat in the lobby and picked up a USA Today to read while he waited. It wasn't long before a young man of about twenty-five exited the elevator, looked around, and saw the receptionist point in Patrick's direction, and he walked over.

"Hi, I'm Allen Goldstein with the news division. Can I help you with something?" he asked.

Patrick stood and folded the newspaper and said, "Mr. Goldstein, if you are with Tom Roberts' show, I think we can help each other."

Ninety minutes later, Patrick walked into the Athena Greek Restaurant to find Bart chatting with the manager, and the two of them laughing. Bart introduced the two and explained that he had eaten there many times over the last three years and said they have the best souvlaki and baklava in town.

Spiro, the nickname of the manager, was actually Italian, and his name was Pietro, but Spiro seemed to fit him just fine. The manager excused himself to return to the kitchen, and Patrick and Bart sat down to discuss the visit to NBC.

"It went even better than expected," Patrick said excitedly.

"Apparently, your Senator Chapman has ruffled a few feathers with news people in this town. Sounds like he's a bit of a bully," he added.

Bart acknowledged this assessment with a nod of his head. "Specifically, the last time he was on Meet the Press, he actually gave Tom Roberts a list of questions he could ask, and when Roberts told him *it doesn't work that way*, the good Senator threatened to walk out of the interview. He was peddling some foreign relations legislation and wanted to control the narrative."

Bart said, "I know exactly what you're talking about. He co-authored a Bill to allow Chinese imports to come in without tariffs for products not produced domestically. It was a trade expansion Bill, but critics said it was too one-sided and enabled China to unfairly increase their exports to the US while not addressing the tariffs on American goods in China. Essentially, it was believed that, if passed, it would increase our Trade Deficit by several hundred billion dollars. Senators Chapman and Gonzales of California, the co-author, argued that it would help the US economy by saving consumers, enabling higher domestic sales, and thereby generating additional tax revenues."

Patrick was surprised and amused. He said, "You really know your stuff, don't you."

Bart smiled confidently and said, "I pay attention. That's the reason I was always so helpful to Senator Chapman and became his top aide pretty quickly. It's also the reason I'm going to take him down. Attention to detail."

"Everything is in place, but Tom Roberts insists on meeting with you personally – just the two of you – to make one hundred percent certain this is on the up and up. You decide where and when, but it needs to be soon so there is time. The show airs at ten am, but the interview with Senator Chapman will be shot at 8 am and then played back on the show, to give them time for edits if necessary."

Patrick continued, "My advice is to do it somewhere away from here so there is less chance of someone recognizing Tom, or you for that matter. Your resurrection needs to be a complete surprise."

Bart smiled and said, "Jews don't believe in resurrections, but we love surprises."

## CHAPTER 15

The Library of Congress had the largest collection of books in the western hemisphere, with over half a million rare books, many of them sold to the library by Thomas Jefferson after it was almost destroyed during the War of 1812.

The Library is a beautifully ornate building with Gilded Age architecture that housed more than twenty-six million books. As a Library Card holder, Bart had access to private reading rooms and chose one of the rooms in the Jefferson Building to meet with Tom Roberts.

A quiet knock on the door to reading room J22 was answered by Bart, and the newsman known for his hard-hitting questioning stepped inside. Pictures of Bartholomew Kroonenberg had circulated since his disappearance thirty-six days earlier. It was the story of the hour a month ago, and nobody could offer any answers, only prayers and good wishes.

The man standing before Roberts at the moment bore some resemblance, but he was completely bald and wore facial hair, which was never in any of the photographs that had been shared by his family or in the one from his Capitol Hill Identification Card.

Bart extended a hand, which found a firm but reasonable handshake from Roberts. He could see the scrutiny with which he was currently undergoing from the practiced eye of the NBC anchor and Washington Bureau Chief.

"Please, Mr. Roberts, let's sit down, and I'll answer any questions you have."

Bart pulled his wallet from his jacket pocket and pulled three cards out and laid them side-by-side on the conference table. "This is my Pennsylvania driver's license, my Capitol Hill ID, and my Library of Congress Reading Card. I know my appearance is different, but Dr. Rivera has already told you the events of the last month and explained the threat I am facing. Anonymity is of utmost importance until the people behind all of this are stopped."

Tom Roberts looked them over carefully, holding each one up and looking from the photo to the face of the young man sitting in front of him.

He finally said, "Okay, Bartholomew, I believe it's really you. Convince me you didn't take an ill-timed spring break and run off to South Beach."

Bart replied, "Please just call me Bart. From this day forward, the only person who can call me by my full-given name is my dad. Let me tell you a story."

For the next thirty minutes, Bart told Roberts everything that had happened from the time he entered the private dining room at Global Achievements and how he believed, but couldn't prove, the note he handed the Senator had caused the death of Patrick's cousin. He also believed it would have caused harm to his college buddy and the fourth golfer, but he managed to not give their names to the Senator when asked. He believed that that one incident is what made the Senator decide to treat Bart as a Sōngsǎn de yīduān, a loose end.

He believed the Senator had taken him to China for the purpose of having him killed or imprisoned as a spy and erased any evidence of his being there. He also believed, based on what Patrick had shared with him, that two employees of the Centennial Golf Course were murdered and a Herndon, Virginia Police Detective had also been murdered on orders from the Senator, or persons in direct contact with him. All of those beliefs were supported by the interviews the Senator had done since returning from China, in which he lied repeatedly about where Bart was.

"That's it. That's all I have, and I can't prove any of it," Bart said and watched as everything he had just told the experienced investigative reporter was marinating inside his head.

"Oh, there is one other thing; I have letters given to me personally by Hŭa Mīng, The CCP Director of Commerce in Beijing that enabled me to get out of China and back to the United States."

Roberts's eyes got a little wider, and the internal marination stopped cold. "You have travel papers from the Chinese Communist Party Director of Commerce?"

Bart proudly said, "Yes, I do. I worked with her for almost three weeks, and she became a very good friend. When all of this is finally over, I want to thank her for all her help, but I'll do it over the phone. I'm never going back to China."

"Are these documents dated? Is there any way to determine their authenticity," he asked.

"I'm not sure if they are dated or not because everything on the page is a Chinese character, but their authenticity is proven because it was the only way we, or I got out of China. Without them, I would still be there. But we can call Hŭa Mīng, and she can verify everything I've just told you," Bart added.

Tom looked at him and seemed a little saddened and said, "I'm afraid that won't be possible. Director Mīng and nine others were apparently part of a coup d'état put down by the CCP Military. She was executed with the other participants on Thursday."

Bart was stunned and broken-hearted to learn of her fate. He knew the truth behind the executions, and it had nothing to do with an attempted take-over of the government. Hŭa Mīng and Quàn Shū were proud and loyal party members, and, though he didn't know the others who were killed, he suspected the same was true of them. They simply failed to deliver the Olympic Games to their paramount leader, and just like the powerful politician he was up against, he was a brutal thug in a Brooks Brothers suit.

Bart and Tom spoke for thirty more minutes until a light came on in the room, indicating his reserved time was up. Bart promised to be at the NBC studio office at six am, two hours ahead of the scheduled interview for which he was certain the Senator would be early. He also promised to bring the documents given to him by the CCP Director of Commerce. There were two stories worth telling, and Roberts intended to tell them. They covered some questions he should ask the Senator and shook hands before exiting the reading room in two different directions.

CHAPTER 16

Bart and Patrick arrived at the NBC studio at five-thirty and drove around the block. Finding a parking garage a block away, they parked on an upper deck where no other cars were parked. Bart was sporting his shiny bald head look with a neatly trimmed beard and mustache. He had also picked up a pair of clear-lensed glasses that completed his unrecognizable appearance. He wore jeans and a polo shirt.

Patrick was dressed in a business suit and looked like he was going to be interviewed on camera. They walked to an employee entrance on E Street NW and waited for ten minutes before the door was opened from the inside by Allen Goldstein, the Producer Patrick had met with the previous day. Allen walked them to a dressing room where Tom was getting ready for his show.

The studio was a beehive of activity with more than twenty people running around preparing for the show and several others setting up an interview stage that resembled a well-appointed law office, complete with bookshelves and photos of presidents on the wall, as well as an American Flag with a gold eagle atop the pole. A small cherry wood table and two comfortable, low-back chairs completed the look.

Three cameras were positioned, with one on each chair to be occupied by Tom and his interviewee, and a third sat ten feet back from the table to capture the full shot of both parties. A red light was mounted on top of each camera, and at the Director's signal, the camera angle would change, and the red light would illuminate to indicate which camera to look into.

Bart and Patrick went over their final instructions with Tom and helped themselves to coffee and other refreshments provided for the staff and visitors of the show. A few minutes past seven am, a booming baritone voice could be heard entering the front of the studio from the lobby elevator. Bart and Patrick quickly moved to the spots Tom had assigned them during the prerecorded interview.

Senator Chapman strolled in, and an aide stood by his side, holding his briefcase and a stainless-steel coffee cup. Bart recognized the aide as Carlotta Jameson, a young woman who had joined the senator's staff in December of the previous year, after the last election, because she had proven herself to be very resourceful and capable in his Richmond re-election office.

Bart was more concerned that she might recognize him than he was about the Senator. She looked around but didn't pay any special attention to Bart.

Instead, she walked over to Patrick and asked, "Who are you?"

Patrick responded coldly, "Not interested," and stepped away, as though she had tried to hit on him. She got red-faced and returned to where she had stood before, then followed the Senator to a makeup chair, where a technician worked on his thick, silver hair and then dabbed powder on his forehead and nose, making sure he had no shiny surfaces that might glare in the studio lights. The Senator joked with the woman applying makeup and seemed as jovial as Bart had ever seen him.

Tom Roberts stepped into the room and shook hands with Senator Chapman, welcoming him back to the NBC studio. He said they would have some preliminary questions in the A block, the first segment, and then, after the first break, during the B block, they would talk about the passage of the Welfare Reform Bill in the House and what Senator Chapman believed would happen when it arrives in the Senate.

Senator Chapman cleared his throat and said, "My assistant has some questions we want to use," and looked in the mirror, saying, "Carlotta, honey, can you give those questions to Tom here?"

Carlotta stepped forward, opened the top of the briefcase, pulled out a sheet of paper, and handed it to Tom Roberts. He looked it over but didn't comment on the self-serving nature of the questions, as he had no intention of asking them.

"Are we all set, Tom?"

"Absolutely, Senator Chapman. I'll see you in the studio when you're ready to get started. Thanks again for being on the show today."

The heat and glare from the key lights, backlights, and base lights were pretty intense, as they had to be to produce a perfectly clear picture for the television viewer. They generated so much ambient heat that oversized air conditioning vents were necessary to cool the studio so people could tolerate them. They also made people being interviewed by Tom Roberts feel like they were literally in the hot seat.

Tom had asked a crew member to close off the air conditioning vent above the seat where the Senator would be sitting. He also had a stainless-steel pitcher of ice water and two glasses on the table, a prop he had never used prior to this interview.

The interview was set to begin, and three cameramen took their places in seats behind large Sony video cameras set on tracks that could be moved into various positions. Beneath each one was a teleprompter from which Tom Roberts would read intermittently, looking from them to his notes to directly into the eyes of the person he was interviewing.

The interview was being recorded for playback, so there was no delay for a commercial break after Tom Roberts talked them out of a segment, and there was no playing of the unmistakable theme song, "The Pulse of Events," which had played for the forty-nine years of the show's run. Those features would be added before playback by an engineer.

The Director of the show was off-stage in a control room, as experienced technicians responded immediately to his directions. They zoomed in a camera for a close-up, switched camera views, overlaid with chyrons (the messaging that scrolls across the bottom of the screen) or with identifiers of a guest so the audience knew who they were, the party and state they represented, and other pertinent information to enhance the informative nature of the show for the viewing public.

A producer on stage counted down from five, four, three, two, one, and then pointed to Tom Roberts, who said, "Good morning from our nation's capital. I'm Tom Roberts, and if it's Sunday, it's Meet The Press."

"Cut!" was heard over the studio intercom. "Camera two set to seven and zoom to one and a quarter." The camera on which Bart was sitting used the camera's body and lens to partially hide his face. It rolled to within seven feet of the table, and he turned the lens to one and a quarter.

"Perfect. Count down," came the voice again, and the producer counted down and pointed to Tom.

"Welcome back to Meet the Press. We are joined by Senator John Chapman of Virginia, Chairman of the Foreign Relations Committee, as well as being a member of the Commerce Committee. Senator, welcome back, and thanks for being here."

"Thank you for having me, Tom. I always appreciate the opportunity to speak with the American people," the

Senator smoothly said, his deep baritone voice being modulated in the control room to prevent buzzing in television speakers in homes, as he looked directly into the camera.

"Senator, we have a lot of very important things to talk about this morning, not the least of which is the Bill coming over from the Republican-controlled House this coming week with sweeping welfare reforms. But I would be remiss if I didn't follow up on something we discussed several weeks ago."

The Senator's eyes narrowed slightly because Tom Roberts had just gone off-script, and he had not expected whatever he was about to ask.

"You have a staff member who went missing over a month ago, and I know how difficult it has been for you. I just wanted to see how you're doing. Have the police or FBI been able to figure out what happened to this young man? Any update at all, sir?"

Clearly relieved, the Senator cleared his throat and said, "I wish there were some news. You know, I haven't said so in past interviews, but that young man, Bartholomew, was like a son to me. He was an invaluable help to me, and he has been difficult to replace. I remain ever hopeful that the authorities will find this young man and bring him back. You know, ours is a rough and draining business, doing the work of the people, and I know that sometimes, the pressure can affect people in unexpected ways." The Senator delivered this little soliloquy with the appearance of true compassion.

"Are you saying you think this man ran off? Succumbed to the pressure of the job and left town? Is that a working theory, Senator Chapman?" Tom asked.

"Well, I can't speak to any direction the investigation is going. I can only surmise that, given the difficult nature of the load and the hours these young people must work in the performance of their duties. You know, they are performing a service to the American people every day, and I, for one, am just so proud of these young folks." Senator Chapman looked at Tom as if to say, *enough is enough*, but Tom wasn't finished.

"Would it surprise you to know that clues have been found that lead to a different possibility, Senator Chapman?" With that, Tom pulled three cards out from a folder lying in front of him. Camera three zoomed into the tabletop to show the three cards as Tom spread them out for clear viewing.

Camera two zoomed to one point five at the Director's instruction, conveyed via a headset worn by Bart.

"This is the driver's license, Capitol ID, and a Library card for your missing aide, Bart Kroonenberg. Were you aware these items had been turned in here in Washington, DC, Senator?"

"Well, of course, I am keeping apprised of the investigation as much as the police are willing to share. But, as I say, it is an ongoing investigation, so…"

"Senator, you recently had a fact-finding visit to mainland China, isn't that right?"

"Yes, as part of my responsibility with respect to the Commerce Committee and in the interest of my Virginia constituency, I have visited China several times, as well as Ireland and Argentina. I even went to Canada," the Senator managed a fake little laugh. "What's your question, Tom?"

"Would it surprise you to know that Bart Kroonenberg, your missing aide, was spotted in Beijing at the same time you were there?" Tom pounced, the camera was tight, and the heat was intense from the lights and the question.

"Well, yes, it would surprise me. Why would you ask such a question? You think my aide managed to get to mainland China without me knowing about it?"

"No, Senator Chapman. I don't think that at all. But I'll tell you what I know. I know that the three pieces of identification you see on the table in front of you were, in fact, in China less than a week ago. There is no question they belong to your missing aide. I also know this: as the current co-chairman of the Senate Commerce Committee, when you visit a foreign land, whether it is an ally or not, you meet with your counterpart in that host nation, in addition to any industrialists or manufacturers you might meet with while there."

Tom pulled a sheet of folded paper from the folder and laid it on the table, saying, "According to this document from The Director of Commerce for the CCP, you didn't meet with her. How do you explain that, Senator?"

This, of course, was a bluff, but the travel documents Bart had shown him were not readable unless the Senator understood Chinese calligraphy.

Senator Chapman sat back and looked like he might be sick. He reached for the mic pack on his belt, but then Tom Roberts said, "Would it surprise you to know that Mr. Kroonenberg, your missing aide, is alive and well, Senator?"

"You're damned right it would surprise me. That boy was suicidal. I haven't said anything before now because I wanted to spare his family. But when I said the pressure was getting to him, that was an understatement. Now this interview is over. Get this thing off of me. I'm all tangled up," the Senator said as he tried to pull the microphone pack off the back of his belt. Tom motioned for the man operating camera number two to come over and disconnect the Senator's microphone, which was still live.

The man stepped forward and began to try to unclip the microphone, and Tom said, "Senator, if you think Bart Kroonenberg may have killed himself, how do you explain his identification cards being in China?"

"How should I know what a crazy person might do? Maybe he mailed them to China. Maybe he stuck them in someone's luggage."

The smiling cameraman said, "Or maybe he traveled with you to Beijing at your request after you ordered the killing of Dr. Robert Rivera on May 28th."

The Senator turned sharply on the cameraman, and with his icy, deep baritone voice, he said, "How dare you make such a salacious accusation! I will have your…"

He stopped mid-sentence and nearly choked on his own breath as he recognized the voice and face that stared at him.

"You'll have my what, Senator Chapman? My life? The lives of my friends? What else can you take from me?"

Bart began removing the stick-on mustache and beard and the glasses, and camera three pulled back and showed all three men perfectly in frame.

The Senator was visibly shaken, and Tom Roberts had a victorious smile as he said, "Ladies and gentlemen of our viewing audience, this is the missing aide, Bart Kroonenberg."

Bart looked like he was close to tears out of sheer anger. "I was loyal to you, Senator. I worked morning, noon, and night for you and never once complained or succumbed to the pressure as you put it. I dropped everything I was doing and flew off to China with you, and you sent that man to kill me. To erase my existence!"

"Son, let me explain."

"Don't call me son. My father has that right. You threw me away, and the things you did have to be answered for."

Patrick stepped forward from behind Camera one, and the Senator glanced over, having no idea who he was or why he was there.

"This is Dr. Patrick Rivera," said Tom Roberts, and the Senator's eyes grew larger, and he seemed to have forgotten that he wanted to be released from his microphone.

"I don't, uh, I'm not. He is uh,"

"Dead? Senator Chapman. Is that what you were going to say?" asked Patrick.

"Don't worry, Senator. I'm not that Dr. Rivera. You did kill him. I'm his cousin, and I'm going to see that you pay for his murder."

"It wasn't me; it was…"

Carlotta stepped forward and asked the Senator to stop talking. She jerked the microphone pack off his belt and threw it and the lapel microphone on the table.

"We're leaving," she announced and led the elderly Senator out by the arm.

They went to the elevator, and Bart walked behind them, saying, "This isn't over, Senator Chapman. Official charges will be filed against you this morning. You won't get away with any of this. You and your friends at Global Achievements are going down."

## CHAPTER 17

The doors closed on the elevator, and Senator Chapman was going down - to the lobby and out to a waiting Town car. As soon as he settled into the back seat and Carlotta went to the front passenger door, the driver locked the door and instructed Carlotta to find a cab and pulled away from the curb. The driver then raised a window separating the back from the front to allow for privacy.

Senator Chapman pulled out a cellphone and made a call to a Georgetown number. This set off a number of calls to be made, and by the time Chapman reached his home in Georgetown, another Town Car was sitting in front of his house. The driver pulled into the driveway, and the senator asked him to wait because he had a couple of stops to make and needed to get to the airport.

He walked up to the side entry of his palatial brick Georgian home, and the visitor walked a few feet behind him. He had never had the head of Global Achievements in a private meeting, let alone in his home, and it was nerve-racking on top of what he had just been through at NBC. They walked into the library, and Chapman offered a bourbon, which was refused, so he drank alone. He sat and, when asked, described in as much detail as possible what had happened.

When he finished, his visitor stood and walked to the side porch to make a phone call and then rejoined the senator in his library. "It's going to be okay, John. We will take care of this situation, and you will never see that embarrassing debacle on the air."

"You can do that? You have that kind of pull?" he asked.

"Trust me, John. I have that much pull and more. I'll have that drink now if you don't mind."

Senator Chapman got up and went to a crystal decanter to pour another drink. "It's five o'clock somewhere, isn't it?" he said over his shoulder as he matched his own drink with three fingers of Kentucky bourbon in a crystal glass for her. He turned and tried to smile, but he was still sick from the experience and wanted to see how much pull his guest had. Was it possible she could make all of this go away completely?

Eloise Chamberlain of the CDC and Chairwoman of Global Achievements was sitting in a chair across from his own, and he set her glass on a round marble table between them. He picked up his glass and made a toast, as she raised hers to join him.

He said, "Here's to the powerful. May we always stick together, and may we always win," and he took a drink and allowed the amber liquor to warm him as he swallowed it. She raised her glass and said, "Here's to you, Sōngsǎn de yīduān," but didn't take a drink; she just smiled.

"What was that, Chinese?" he asked.

She replied calmly, "Mandarin, John. It's a wonderfully descriptive name. It means, loose end."

He noticed she did not take a drink and asked, "Something wrong with your drink? Would you rath..." The glass fell from his hand, and he looked down and then over at her and said, "I..." then he fell face first into the marble table but was dead before he struck it.

NBC's Meet the Press aired a very damaging interview with Senator John Chapman on Sunday, July 6th, 1996, but as promised, he never saw it hit the airwaves. He was found dead in his home when Georgetown police and Capitol Police arrived at his residence an hour after the program.

Bart and Patrick had left the studio and driven straight to the Georgetown Police Department with a tape of the interview and followed a detective and a patrol car to the senator's residence. A black Town Car sat in the driveway with the driver slumped sideways in the seat, dead from an apparent gunshot wound to his temple.

Police forcibly entered the front door of Senator Chapman's residence and did a sweep of every room, finding the senator's lifeless body in the opulent library at the rear of the first floor. Bart admitted to slipping the recorder into Senator Chapman's pocket while ostensibly removing his mic pack.

He then pulled a Motorola pager from his own pocket and said, "I took this from the senator too. You may find contacts of interest on it. I'd pay special attention to any numbers with nine eleven in the message. He used to get those and ask me to leave the room before returning the call."

The micro recorder found in the dead senator's coat pocket had recorded his side of four telephone calls made from the car and even recorded the brief conversation he had with an unknown woman in his home. It recorded his death collapse and the sound of someone pulling on rubber gloves and clinking glassware, but there was no way to identify who the mystery woman was.

The Capitol Police showed up at the scene, having been sent by the Senate Majority Leader to secure any and all documents in Senator Chapman's possession, and the two agencies were arguing over jurisdiction when Bart and Patrick asked and were permitted to leave. They drove back to the hotel, talking excitedly along the way about what may come next.

"Heads are going to roll, now," said Patrick. "All of his underhanded dealings are going to surface now, and Global Achievements is going to be destroyed."

Bart had been around the true power brokers of Washington DC and had seen the wagons circle to protect their own and wasn't as optimistic as Patrick. Few brokers had as much sway with Senate leadership as did Global Achievements.

"I'm hopeful we can catch a few more fish in the net, especially with the contacts on Senator Chapman's pager. If they find his cellphone, they should have another treasure trove to work with," Bart suggested.

Patrick hoped they would all swing, knowing that the senator and his Global Achievements cronies were behind his cousin's murder, as well as Chain McLarney and his Pro

Shop Manager, Greg Landers. It dawned on him that he should call Detective Williams at the Herndon P.D and bring her up to date. He told Bart as much, and Bart decided they should go see her the following morning.

CHAPTER 18

The drive took a little more than forty-five minutes with traffic, and Bart parked the rental car in a public lot across the street from the Herndon Police Department, just before 7 a.m. Patrick took the lead, and they checked in at the front counter, signing a Visitors Log on a clipboard passed under a plexiglass window, and then sat down on hard plastic seats bolted to rolled metal in the lobby. Several uniformed police officers and a couple of plainclothes detectives, badges displayed on their belts, walked to a door and were buzzed in by the Desk Sergeant beyond the plexiglass.

At 7:15, an African American woman in her mid-forties came in carrying a Starbucks coffee cup and a USA Today newspaper. She was athletically built and a little taller than Patrick, at five feet eleven inches, Patrick guessed. As she reached the door, a buzzer sounded. She strode in, and the Desk Sergeant walked over and spoke with her. She set her coffee and newspaper down, opened the door, and stood holding the doorknob as she said, "I'm Detective Williams. You waiting to see me?"

Patrick and Bart stood quickly, and Patrick spoke. "Detective Williams, I'm Dr. Patrick Rivera," and he noticed a slight upward turn of her eyes.

"Dr. Rivera. I thought I told you two weeks ago we had nothing to talk about."

"Please. Just hear me, hear us out. It will take ten minutes of your time, I promise."

The detective stood and looked at Patrick for an uncomfortable moment and said, "Who's this you have with you?"

"This is Bart Kroonenberg. He is, or was, an aide to Senator Chapman."

The detective's eyes got big, and she stepped out and let the door close. "This just got a little more interesting. You're the guy who went missing a while back, aren't you?" Williams asked.

Bart stepped forward and reached out to shake her hand and replied, "Yes. That's me. Is there someplace we can talk? Like Patrick said, ten minutes is all we need."

"I'll give you five, and we start with where you have been hiding and why. Follow me," she led them back to the door, waited for the buzz and click, and stepped through.

They followed her to an interview room across a narrow walkway from a group of cubicles with low walls and high-backed office chairs, where three other plainclothes cops were laughing at something one of them had said, which Bart nor Patrick heard, but Williams did. She flipped them the finger over her shoulder and walked into the small interview room.

There was a camera in two of the corners at ceiling height, and when Detective Williams asked Bart to shut the door, he noticed a green light come on at both. Williams saw him looking and said, "Everything is on the record here."

Bart took a seat at the table next to Patrick and across from Detective Williams, and Patrick said, "When we last spoke," and Detective stopped him with a raised palm.

"You and I may have more to talk about, but that hasn't been decided yet. I want his story first," she said.

Patrick and Bart looked at each other and then at the detective, and Bart said, "My story starts in the same place Patrick's does, with the murder of his cousin and the subsequent murders of two people at a golf course and the murder of one of your detectives, all at the hands, or at least the orders, of Senator John Chapman."

The detective looked at Bart and Patrick and just smiled and shook her head and said, "OK. You got me. I want to hear this. Don't leave anything out. If you're going to convince me that a man who died yesterday can just about clear my wall, I'm all in. But don't think you're going to play me."

Bart laid it all out for her, and Patrick contributed to the dialogue as best he could, explaining what he and Gary Saunders had talked about and the strange happenings that resulted in his cousin being cremated. They told her about the interview with Tom Roberts and the sting operation Tom had orchestrated to trip the senator up.

Detective Williams had not seen the interview entirely, but thirty-second sound bites had played on all the television news services with the news of the senator's death. Capitol Police and Georgetown police were not releasing any details about his death, but Bart and Patrick told her that his driver had been murdered in the driveway, so there was no way it could be anything but a murder.

"You think the senator murdered his driver, then killed himself?" she sneered.

Bart said, "No. I think someone else murdered both of them. I planted a microcassette recorder in the senator's pocket at the NBC studio, and I pocketed his pager. The playback at the senator's house revealed several calls he made and talked openly about the killing of Patrick's cousin and the nosey cop that was getting too close."

Patrick added, "Gary Saunders was the only cop he could have been talking about, and if the same guy killed Gary and Patrick, it makes sense that the same person killed Mr. McLarney and the guy in the pro shop at Centennial."

Detective Williams had taken it all in and had finally come to realize Bart and Patrick were not crazy, but she said, "You still haven't answered my question. Where have you been, and why the hide and seek?"

Bart smiled and said, "That's an interesting story with a happy ending," and for the next ten minutes, he told her in detail about what had happened and how he had been saved by Hǔa Míng and Yún Lǐ. When he had finished, the detective looked at the two men a little differently than she had when she first met them twenty minutes earlier.

"Wait here a minute. I want you to look at something," and she got up and left the room. She returned a minute later with a laptop computer and a clear, plastic evidence envelope. She pulled a CD out of the envelope and slid it into the side of the computer after a lengthy start-up process. The CD began to play, and the detective now stood behind Bart and Patrick.

She pointed at the screen and said, "This is surveillance footage from two businesses at an off-ramp on I-95 between here and Richmond, on the northbound side of the Interstate. The first segment is from an AMOCO station, and it's a little grainy and it's black and white."

They watched as a semi-tractor-trailer pulled to a stop sign and made a wide right turn on the access road heading north, and then a light sedan pulled up to the stop sign in the northbound direction, having exited the freeway. It signaled to turn right, most likely to turn into the gas station where the camera was located.

A dark SUV pulled up beside the sedan and then pulled away and turned left. The light sedan started rolling slowly forward across the lane and up onto the curb and grassy area in front of the gas station, and suddenly exploded into a bright fireball that flared white across the lens for several seconds.

Then the next segment started to play, and Williams said, "This is from a dry cleaner on the other side of the underpass, and we have it synchronized to the exact time as the black and white. This place is one hundred ninety feet from the burning vehicle."

They watched, and for twenty seconds, nothing happened other than a Volkswagen coming down the Southbound ramp and making a right turn. Then the dark SUV, they could now see that it was black, came under the overpass and stopped at a traffic light for a few seconds. Over the top of the overpass, a cloud of smoke and fire could be seen. Then the car turned left and headed south on I-95.

"Wow. What did we just watch?" Bart asked, and Patrick knew exactly what it was.

"That was the murder of Detective Gary Saunders," answered Patrick.

"Yes, it was," echoed Detective Williams. "If I slow down the black and white, you can see a muzzle extend from the window, then two flashes, and then something being thrown from the SUV into Gary's car. Our forensic people say it was a phosphorus grenade. Haven't seen one since I was in the Marines in Desert Storm. Used them to clear caves sometimes. The two muzzle flashes have to mean Gary was shot or shot at twice. There were no slugs on the scene and there was nothing left but ashes from his knees up, so nothing to find there," she added.

Patrick was visibly upset, and he said, "This was hard to watch. Why did you show us these videos?"

"The part I really want to show you is coming up." The screen went black for a few seconds, and then the full-color video restarted at the point the black SUV pulled up to the stoplight. Then it zoomed in very close and was too blurry to make out anything, and then it zoomed out some and then a little more until a face could be seen in the passenger seat of the car. The face was too blurred to make out any significant detail, but the occupant appeared to be short with short dark hair.

"Looks like that guy Tang or Tong I told you about, Patrick," Bart said.

"Looks a little like the guy that came into the pool area at my hotel in Reston. Remember me telling you about that?" Bart did and said, could be the same guy.

Williams wrote something on her steno pad and said, "How about this," and she pointed to a windshield sticker on the car that was blown up to five hundred percent on the screen and frozen.

"We have been looking through catalogs and online databases for any organization with a six alpha or six pyramid symbol, and we have come up blank."

Bart knew instantly what it was because he had seen them dozens of times while working for the senator. He said, "It isn't a six. That's a G and that's an A. It's a parking sticker for Global Achievements. And that SUV is just like the ones they use for company vehicles."

Detective Williams wrote down how she could reach Bart and Patrick and thanked them for the information they had provided as she walked them out. They drove back into Washington DC and checked out of the hotel. Bart was anxious to get back to his parents' house and to Yún.

It took a while tidying up his room the way his parents had always told him to do, and a moment of clarity came to him. He had picked a towel up from the floor and stopped, went to the phone on the bedside table and called Detective Williams.

"The guy in the photo. His name is Tau, I'm sure of it. Doctor Lǐ Xìng Taū."

Patrick had an open-ended ticket and called the airlines and booked a flight for that night out of Philadelphia. They used the three-hour drive to talk and learn about each other. Bart had never met the late Dr. Rivera, but he enjoyed hearing stories about their relationship, and it seemed like they were as close as brothers. That made Bart think of his older brother and his sister and made a mental note to reconnect as quickly as possible.

His three years in Washington DC working the demanding job of supporting a United States Senator had left no time for family, and with the limited time he had, he managed to stay in touch with his mom and dad. He vowed to correct that. They both felt as though their circumstances had brought them together, and they each had a friend for life, in spite of the argument they had for over an hour on the drive about who was better, the Dallas Cowboys or The Philadelphia Eagles. They decided on that matter, they would just agree to disagree.

## TYING UP SŌNGSĂN DE YĪDUĀN (LOOSE ENDS)

Detective Lisa Williams was able to lead a Task Force that included the FBI and the ATF in bringing several high-level individuals to justice. Following up on information she got from Patrick and Bart, Detective Williams talked to the General Manager at the Hilton Hotel where Patrick had stayed and was directed to the franchise main office in Richmond. She spoke with their head of security, Ken Vogel, who wondered why it had taken so long for someone to follow up. He had been holding onto video evidence for Detective Saunders for more than a month.

The video from the Hilton was clear, in full color, and helped to identify the Asian man who had entered the Hilton Exercise Center as Lĭ Xìng Taū. Detective Williams also pulled surveillance video from the Marriott hotel from the morning Dr. Rivera was murdered, and Tau was recorded in the lobby and the entrance to the Breakfast Room and climbing into a Silver Infinity SUV with a Global Achievements parking decal in the left corner of the windshield.

Lĭ Xing Taū was not a doctor but had experience as a lab assistant and was listed with the State Department as being in the United States consulting with the Centers for Disease Control on a temporary Work Visa, which had expired. He was the head of Security for Global Achievements Chinese Subsidiary in Wuhan, China. Further investigation showed direct financial ties between Global Achievements and a lab located in Wuhan that was being run by the brother of Tau. Lǐ Xing Taū was arrested in his Security Office at Global Achievements and, four days later, was found dead in his cell at the Fairfax County Jail of an apparent heart attack.

The voice on the recording from the microcassette recorder placed in Senator John Chapman's coat pocket was never identified but given the involvement of Global Achievements in the four murders, the Chairwoman of the company, Eloise Chamberlain, vowed the full support of her company and their security services. The offer was made in writing, as Ms. Chamberlain had laryngitis the day Detective Williams met with her, and the Detective declined the offer, feeling like Global Achievements' involvement in the case had created enough problems.

Telephone records for the late senator revealed that he had called Grant Hofstetter, a Project Manager with Global Achievements as well as the Security Office for Global Achievements, but there was nothing that showed who answered the call at the Security Office.

Grant Hofstetter agreed to turn State's Witness in exchange for Immunity and protection, but the day his attorney was to accompany him to the Herndon Police Department, he found the sixty-two-year-old Hofstetter had hung himself in his garage wearing a suit and bowtie.

No other charges came out of the case, but Detective Lisa Williams was satisfied that of the cases that covered her wall and kept her up at night, four of them were closed. She had added Dr. Patrick Rivera to her case load as an open murder investigation and was able to get the County Coroner to change the death certificate, and when the case was solved she made a point of contacting all of the Drs. Rivera to let them know.

Detective Williams also stopped by the Centennial Golf Course to speak with the son of Chain McLarney. She was met by Carrie Darling who had returned to work to keep the Course functioning under the new leadership of Dave McLarney. They were relieved to know the murders had been solved. Detective Williams noticed a bucket truck at the entrance of the Centennial parking lot working on the Centennial pole sign, and there were painters working on two walls of the lobby and asked Carrie and Dave what changes were being made. Dave had changed the name and was putting up new signage for The Chain Links Golf Course, in honor of his father.

Bart returned to Philadelphia, where he and Yún Lǐ married six months later. Bart got involved in state politics and eventually ran for a United States Congressional seat, as a Republican. A black man running for office as a Republican in Pennsylvania was not easily accepted, but in 2012, Pennsylvania elected a Republican Governor, and Bart Kroonenberg succeeded in his third campaign and went to Washington DC as a Freshman in the 112th Congress, determined to make a difference.

Yún Lǐ finished her art degree at Moore College of Art and Design and opened a studio in Haddonfield, a suburb of Philadelphia and close to the home where she and Bart and their three children live. Their eldest daughter, Hŭa

Mīng "Lacy" Kroonenberg recently graduated with honors from Villanova with a degree in Political science. Their son, Quàn Shū is a freshman at Harvard, and Patrick Lee, their youngest son is a sophomore in high school. Their lives have been rich and fulfilled, and they have never brushed against the type of evil that brought Bart and Yún together.

Bart and Patrick remain close and visit one another every year when the Eagles play the Cowboys, in whichever city they play.

In December of 2019, for the first time since that horrible period in 1996, Bart began to see some of the faces and hear some of the names from that horrible time so long ago. The news started airing stories about a virus coming out of China.

The President of the United States had some concerns about it spreading to the US, but he said, initially, there was nothing for Americans to worry about. The virus was thought to have originated from a wet market in Wuhan, China, but some reports indicated that it may have come from a lab there.

The Director of the Wuhan Laboratory, Lǐ Chu Taū vehemently denied the lab had anything to do with the creation of deadly viruses. Other reports speculated about a possible connection to the CCP and the Chinese military.

Dr. Anthony Foster of the CDC spoke to the American people and assured them that if everyone simply washed their hands for thirty seconds several times each day and wore a surgical mask, like one he held up for the cameras, and stand six feet apart at all times and stayed home for just fourteen days, the virus would die and just go away.

When Bart and Yún raised a glass of champagne and toasted the incoming new year on December 31, 2019, they kissed and looked to the sky over a nearby park where fireworks were on display. As they walked back in from the patio to watch the Times Square celebration, Yún said, "today begins the new Chinese year too, Bar." Bart still loved the intentional mispronunciation of his name that only Yún could get away with.

"What is it now? Year of the dragon? Year of the tiger?" he asked with a huge smile that expressed how happy he was with the life they had built together.

"Not even close, Bar. It's the Year of the Rat." Bart's smile faded.

Epilogue

In January of 2020, the President issued a travel ban and his opponents, which was every Democrat politician in America, the national press, the Intelligence Services, and the Department of Justice, began saying he was racist and xenophobic for restricting who could come into the country.

By late February, the number of sick and dying began to be reported on a daily basis and the Administration started having daily Covid 19 briefings with Dr. Foster and Dr. Eloise Chamberlain speaking from the White House podium, answering questions, and giving American's much needed information about how to survive the deadly virus.

Word of the Wuhan laboratory's possible involvement was discredited and the Director, Doctor Lĭ Chu Taū was built up to be a hero for having discovered the virus had come from nature and had spread from the wet market. The wet market was closed down and all of the booths were burned to the ground and some of the merchants were put into work camps.

The President formed a White House Council to tackle the effects and the damages the spreading virus was causing, with Operation Lightning Rod, which streamlined the path from microscope to market for a vaccine and was able to get one out for the public in nine months, shaving three years off the normal requirement for FDA approval.

Therapeutics and vaccines were developed by three of the largest Pharmaceutical companies in America, including Warner Labs in Richardson, Texas where their

Director of Development, Dr. Patrick Rivera was first to market with an effective vaccine and booster.

The President enacted the Defense Production Act (DPA), bringing auto, air conditioning and other manufacturers under control of the government to produce much needed ventilators for hospitals and within thirty days they were supplying hospitals all over the country who blamed the high death count on a lack of ventilators for patients.

He brought textile and clothing manufactures under the authority of the DPA to produce the masks Dr. Anthony Foster said were needed by every human being on the planet. Dr. Foster gave orders for American suppliers to use masks produced in China and the ones being produced in America were then sent around the world to countries who were dangerously low on masks, ventilators, hospital beds and places to bury their dead.

Dr. Foster issued an order in April of 2020 that people could not visit sick relatives who were hospitalized with the virus. He issued another order forbidding people to attend funerals for the loved ones who passed away. He further isolated the American people with orders to not attend church services as places of worship were added to the list of "Super Spreader Events" and asked that people report their neighbors who violated the order.

The government began to operate as though they had an open checkbook, paying people to stay home and issuing orders for non-essential businesses to close down. Restaurants, bars, barber and beauty shops, oil change businesses, dry cleaners every imaginable small and medium business closed down, and many of them never reopened. The only businesses who thrived during the pandemic were Amazon and Walmart, both of whose stock played an important role in Dr. Anthony Fosters portfolio.

Landlords were forbidden to evict tenants for non-payment even those tenants who continued to work or who were actually making more money than ever via enhanced unemployment benefits and government stimulus checks.

There was a brief moment in time when Americans seemed to have a "we're in it together" attitude, much like after the towers fell in 2001, but that feeling soon faded as tensions were constantly high due to isolation and loneliness.

Children were kept home from school and schools began teaching children remotely via zoom meetings which resulted in a severe decline in their learning. Aptitude tests fell to an all-time low, as children struggled to learn from mask covered faces and not being with friends. The worst result of all was the suicide rate amongst children and adults sky-rocketed.

The Governor of New York issued an order to move virus afflicted elderly people into unprotected nursing homes instead of hospitals, resulting in the deaths of thousands of elderly who had not previously been ill. The death toll climbed so rapidly the dead were warehoused in freezers for months before they could be buried.

The virus attacked the elderly, the infirmed, the obese and people with co-morbidity like diabetes, heart ailments and kidney disease. It killed people over sixty-five at a rate in excess of ninety percent of those afflicted. Those younger American's with co-morbidity had a death rate over twenty percent.

Everyone who spoke in opposition to the president continued to lavish praise on Dr. Anthony Foster who boastfully called himself "Science" while insisting that everyone in America should simply shut up and follow the science. The pandemic was used as a weapon against the president who lost his reelection bid to a former peer of Senator John Chapman.

The new president spoke only in favor of everything Dr's Foster and Chamberlain recommended, in spite of the evidence which said they were dead wrong in every step they had taken along the way. It was discovered that they were using the steps taken by the government in 1918 when the Spanish Influenza pandemic ravaged the country and the world. It wasn't an effective response in 1918 and it wasn't more than one hundred years later.

The deceit and corruption around the pandemic had been rampant, with Hospitals falsifying the cause of death to qualify for government funding, business owners accepting government support PPP money and as always, fraud within Medicare and Medicaid were out of control.

But one thing happened that had been predicted or planned for in a meeting in Reston, Virginia in 1996. Due to deaths from the virus, the number of people on Social Security and Medicare was reduced by more than twenty percent, making both programs more viable and extending the lives of the programs a little longer. For the two programs to truly succeed well into the future, with the tentacles of government reaching in to pull from the Social Security Trust Fund for every imaginable pet project, another, more deadly pandemic will be required. Baby boomer recipients outnumber the generation of workers contributing to the fund, so the elderly problem will need to be addressed again. The fine folks at Global Achievements, with their friends in Wuhan, Tehran, and the White House, are already working on a solution.

The End

If you enjoyed The Year of the Rat, please let me know by leaving a review on Amazon: The Year of the Rat

Made in the USA
Columbia, SC
07 February 2025